D0960334

I AM CANADA

Shot at Dawn

World War I

by John Wilson

Scholastic Canada Ltd.

Toronto New York London Auckland Sydney
Mexico City New Delhi Hong Kong Buenos Aires

A Dear Canada book. Published by Scholastic Canada Ltd.
SCHOLASTIC and I AM CANADA and logos are trademarks
and/or registered trademarks of Scholastic Inc.

Library and Archives Canada Cataloguing in Publication

Wilson, John (John Alexander), 1951-
Shot at dawn : World War I / John Wilson.

(I am Canada)
ISBN 978-0-545-98595-6

1. Canada. Canadian Army--History--World War, 1914-1918--Juvenile fiction.
2. World War, 1914-1918--Desertions--Canada--Juvenile fiction.
3. Courts-martial and courts of inquiry--Canada--Juvenile fiction. I. Title.
II. Series: I am Canada

PS8595.I5834S56 2011   jC813'.54   C2010-906024-5

6 5 4 3 2 1   Printed in Canada   114   11 12 13 14 15

The display type was set in Roman Antique.
The text was set in Minion.

First printing January 2011

MIX
From responsible
sources
FSC™ C016245
www.fsc.org

In memory of Private S/14143,
Richard Symons Hay, 7th Battalion,
Queen's Own Cameron Highlanders.
Killed in action, 25th September, 1915,
Battle of Loos, France

Prologue

Outside Amiens, August 23, 1918

In the fading light, the officer strides across the floor of the quarry towards the ramshackle wooden hut, the gravel rattling under his boots. He tries to keep his eyes fixed on the ground in front of him, but they keep being drawn to his right where a solid wooden post is embedded in the ground. Eventually he stops walking, sighs and turns to stare at the stake. The memory is too vivid to be denied. He closes his eyes, but the scene plays itself out on the back of his eyelids.

It is dawn, some three months earlier, in a different quarry several miles to the north. A boy, no more than eighteen years old, is being half dragged, half carried towards a similar post. He is sobbing uncontrollably.

Ten men stand with their backs to the post, fidgeting nervously. Ten rifles lie on the ground before them.

The boy is tied to the post. He has to be tied tightly because he keeps sliding down onto his knees. A bag

1

is placed over his head, muffling his sobs, and a rectangular envelope is pinned over his heart.

An order is given and the men bend, pick up a rifle each and turn to face the boy.

Another order. They aim.

A third order. A flock of crows in the neighbouring field rises in raucous flight at the rifles' report.

The boy's head is slumped forward; his sobbing has stopped. Three ragged holes puncture his chest. No one hit the envelope.

The soldiers rest their rifles on their shoulders, turn and march out of the quarry. Two of them are weeping silently.

The officer realizes that it was his voice that gave the orders.

"Damn this war to hell," he mutters under his breath as he continues his journey to the shed. He unholsters his pistol and hands it to the guard outside for safekeeping. He opens the door.

"Am I to be shot?" The voice comes from the thicker darkness where a shadowy figure can just be made out, sitting at a rough table beneath a grubby window in the rear wall. The air smells stale and dusty.

"I don't know," the officer says, stepping forward. He stands, silhouetted in the door frame, waiting for his eyes to adjust to the gloom. He can hear the man breathing.

"If you haven't brought news of my reprieve, then why are you here?" the soldier asks, an edge of bitterness in his voice.

"I'm here so you won't be alone tonight."

"Another guard, more like."

The officer pulls over a chair and sits at the table. He strikes a match and lights the candle that sits between them. In the flickering light he can see the soldier clearly now. He is young, not more than seventeen or eighteen, but his eyes look old.

"It's true, I cannot let you escape, but that's not why I'm here." The officer takes a bottle of rye whiskey from his pocket and places it on the table.

The soldier's gaze flicks over to it and returns to the officer's face. "You think I want to spend my last hours drunk?"

The officer shrugs. "Some do."

"We shoot a lot of our own men, do we?"

"Too many," the officer replies. He holds out his hand. "My name's Paul," he says. "I'm from Sarnia." He hesitates, as if unsure what to say next. "It's the oil capital of Canada."

The soldier stares at Paul's outstretched hand. He sighs. "Listen. Unless a reprieve comes through, in about eight hours they will tie me to that post out there and ten of my fellow soldiers will try to make my suffering as short as possible." His voice quavers.

He closes his eyes and breathes deeply to bring himself back under control.

"I don't want to get drunk," he continues. "I don't want to make small talk and I don't want to hear about Sarnia. But I do want people back home to know what happened."

"If you give me your parents' address, I promise I'll write to them."

"And say what? That their son died bravely for King and Country? They don't need lies about what's going to happen to me here tomorrow. I'm talking about telling the truth so that, maybe, some of this insanity makes sense. I need to record everything that happened to bring me here. Do you have paper and pencil?"

The officer takes a notebook and the stub of a pencil out of his uniform pocket and pushes them across the table.

"Not for me," the soldier says, "for you. You might as well do something worthwhile. You're an officer, you must have had a gentleman's education. Can you write shorthand to dictation?"

The officer nods.

"Good. Then write down everything I say in that notebook. I'm going to tell you a story."

"What sort of story?"

The soldier smiles. "A true story."

Chapter 1

The Calm Before the Storm

Nicola Valley, British Columbia, early years of the war

I grew up on my father's ranch in the Nicola Valley in British Columbia. My dad was Irish, a McBride from outside Dublin. He reckoned that I was crazy wanting to come out to this war.

"What d'you want to fight somebody else's battles for, Allan?" he asked me. "Back in Ireland, they been fighting each other or the English for hundreds of years and a lot of damned good it's done anyone."

I wish I'd listened to him now, but I didn't. You see, my dad and I are very different. He's practical, good at building a fence or shoeing a horse. He thinks his way through a problem. I take after my mom. I do what feels right. A born romantic, that's me. Tales of doomed rebellions against the English and hopeless last stands on top of some forgotten hill could reduce me to tears.

Anyway, come my seventeenth birthday, a year ago last March, I announced I was off to Merritt to get the CPR down to the coast and join up. Mom cried a lot, but Dad just said, "Why?"

Well, that was a tough question.

"I want to see the world," I said. "The Valley's too small and I don't want to be a cowboy or go down the coal mines."

I think my reasons were close enough to those that drove my dad out of Ireland for him to understand and give me his reluctant blessing, but I hadn't told him the truth.

The truth was, I was trying to be Ken Harrison. Ken was four years older than me and he was my hero. He was tall, fair-haired and had a face that seemed always about to break into a broad grin. He grew up on the ranch beside ours and since we were both only boys, we spent a lot of time together. He taught me to fish the lakes for trout before the sun got too high and the ospreys and eagles came out and drove the fish deep, and he showed me the best places to find blue grouse and mule deer.

I became a good hunter. I got to recognize the animals' signs, knew what trails they used and where they would be at certain times of day. I was a good shot, too, but I always let Ken do the killing, at least after that first time.

I was about twelve and Ken had led us up the end of the valley to search for deer. We crawled up a hill and saw four of them below us beside the river. One was a nice buck and, through signs, Ken told me to take the shot.

It was a long shot, but I estimated the distance and set the sights. I aimed for a heart shot — behind the shoulder, just where he'd taught me — and squeezed the trigger.

I don't know if I set the sights wrong or if the kick threw the barrel up, but the bullet went high and caught the deer in the spine about the middle of the back. The hind legs collapsed and it went down, but it was still alive, throwing its head in the air and trying to stand on its front legs.

I didn't think, just ran down the hill. When I got to the deer, it was still struggling, breathing in huge gasps and with strings of snot flying from its nose. Its eyes were bulging and it was making a weird, high-pitched screaming sound. It sounded almost human.

"Finish it," Ken said as he came up behind me.

I raised the rifle and aimed and, almost as if it knew what was going on, the deer stopped struggling. I couldn't look at its eyes, so I closed mine and pulled the trigger.

When I looked, the deer was dead, a small black hole in its head. There was a thin line of smoke rising from the hole.

I threw down the rifle and collapsed, sobbing.

Ken tried to comfort me, but it didn't do any good. For days I moped around, thinking of the dying deer, and for weeks afterwards I was plagued by nightmares. I'd wake up screaming with the vision of that deer's dying look fresh in my mind.

I guess that's the other part of having a romantic soul — sensitivity. After that, I still used to accompany Ken when he went hunting, but the only things I shot at were rocks and trees.

Once we took a couple of ponies and went into the high mountains after sheep. While Ken was working his way into position for a difficult shot, I went off on my own. I climbed too high and fell. The snap my leg made was so loud, you could hear the echo come back off the far valley wall. Ken found me, strapped the leg up and got me down just ahead of the first fall blizzard. He saved my life for sure.

Ken's one of those people who figures life's always simple. You look around, make a decision, live with it and things just seem to turn out. So it was natural when the war came in August of 1914 that he would be one of the first to volunteer.

"Got to go and do my bit," he told me cheerfully. "Can't let the Germans go charging all over Europe invading any country they please. Someone's got to stop them."

"I'll go too," I said.

"You can't, Allan," Ken said with a laugh. "You're too young. Besides, the war'll be over long before you're old enough. To tell you the truth, I'm scared the war'll be over before I get there. Finished by Christmas, they say."

Ken was wrong about that, but then so was nearly everyone else. I spent 1915 and 1916 reading about the war and waiting until I was old enough to join up.

Looking back now, I can't believe that I never once made the connection between the way I felt about shooting a deer and how I might feel having to shoot a man. In the stories that I read, it was always *us* — brave, strong and right — and *them* — evil, twisted and inhuman. I believed every story in the newspapers about wicked, cowardly Huns shooting helpless nuns, nailing Canadian soldiers to church doors and bayonetting babies. No one told me the truth.

Ken came home on leave for Christmas 1916. He was a lieutenant by then and I thought he looked wonderful in his uniform. He said he had had some kind of wound but he was never specific and, much as I nagged him to show me the scar and tell me the story, he never said a word. He did look pale, though, and often when he thought I wasn't watching, he would drift off and his gaze would fix on something in the far distance that I could never see.

He stayed with us for a few days when his parents went up to Kamloops to visit a relative and, at night, I would hear him walking about the house. Once I woke to what I thought was a scream, but I managed to convince myself it was a bird or a rabbit being taken by a weasel.

I pestered Ken to tell me tales of the battles he'd been in, but he only ever told me stories about trips he'd taken to Edinburgh and London, practical jokes he and his friends had played on the quartermaster when the battalion was at rest, and soccer games they played against Scottish regiments. I suppose he did it to protect me, but it backfired. His stories only reinforced my idea that the war was all good fun.

I kept reading reports of battles in the newspapers and worshipping the heroes they talked about. I asked Ken why he hadn't won a medal yet, but he just looked at me sadly and said not everyone could have a medal because then they wouldn't mean anything.

I saw nothing except the view I had gleaned from the books that I grew up reading, the adventure stories of Rider Haggard and Henty. In the pages of books like *King Solomon's Mines* I could trade the confines of the Nicola Valley for the exotic reaches of the Empire. I suppose I thought the war must be like one of my adventure stories. The hero would struggle against adversity, he'd triumph in the end and only the bad guys would die. There was nothing in the papers or in what Ken told me that Christmas to make me think any different.

The day Ken left to go back, I went to the station to see him off.

"I'll come out and help as soon as I can," I blurted as I handed him his kit bag through the carriage window.

A look of almost terror crossed his face before he got himself back under control.

"You stay here and look after the ranch," he said.

The train jerked and started moving down the platform in a cloud of steam. I struggled through the crowd to keep up.

"No way!" I shouted. "You can't have all the excitement. I want to be part of the adventure, too."

Ken shook his head and shouted something back, but it was lost in the scream of the train's whistle. Then he was gone.

Four months after that the newspapers were shouting about how the Canadians had stormed up a place called Vimy Ridge and taken the heights that had defeated the French and British for two years. That decided me. A week later, I was standing in front of the recruiting sergeant in Vancouver and telling him I wanted to join Ken's unit in France. I had to add a year onto my age, but they were so desperate for soldiers, no one questioned it.

The weeks of basic training outside Calgary, the train across the country and the ship over to England and then France are all a blur in my memory. Every day I saw or heard or learned something new, but everything that summer was a part of the old world that doesn't exist anymore. My new world, and my introduction to the hell that has led me to this shed tonight, began the day in September I arrived at Etaples.

Chapter 2
A Brutal Beginning
Etaples, France, September 1917

"Quick march!"
  "Halt!"
  "Right wheel!"
  "Double time!"
Laden like mules and in the face of an incessant, bitter wind off the English Channel, we marched back and forth across the packed sand of the parade ground at Etaples until our feet bled, our muscles seized up and our brains ceased to function in a red haze of exhaustion and pain. Endlessly, we stabbed our bayonets into the guts of hanging straw-filled bags, wrestled each other in hand-to-hand combat and lay terrified in suffocating gas masks while swirling poison filled the air around us. What little time we had to ourselves was spent in wolfing down our rations before collapsing onto our cots for a few hours of oblivion. A few hardy souls braved the military police — the Red Caps, we called them — to sneak over the muddy inlet at low tide to sample the forbidden

pleasures of the local town, but most of us were too exhausted.

Many nights, in the brief moments before I escaped into sleep, my mind flashed back to the Nicola Valley. For an instant I could smell the sage as I walked the dry hills or feel the cool dawn air on my cheek as Ken and I sat by a rock watching a mob of deer pick their way over a mountain slope. At times I almost cried at the sense of loss, but I took comfort from the fact that I was doing my duty and that I would soon be with Ken.

Looking back on it now, I have trouble believing how naïve I was then. Nothing at Etaples was remotely like what I had imagined army life to be. We were fighting for honour and our country in a just cause, and I thought we would be treated as heroes for that. Instead we were pushed to our physical and emotional limit. The training in Canada and England had been hard, but there was a level of brutality at Etaples that none of us had come up against before. Up until then we'd felt that the hardships were for our own good. At Etaples the profanities hurled at us by screaming sergeants and the pointless brutality simply encouraged dissatisfaction and hatred. It was as if the instructors seemed to think we could be motivated to fight the Germans better if Etaples was turned into a hell that made battle appear a blessed relief.

I tried to maintain my spirit and optimism by believing that this was a modern war, different from the glorious cavalry charges I had read about. I could see that training soldiers for this war required different methods. I rationalized that the harsh treatment and brutal conditions were designed to harden us and prepare us for the rigours of the trenches. I was only partially successful, and not everyone felt the way I did.

"I tell you it's bloody well true. First the Russians and now the French have refused to fight. We're the only idiots left who are dying so the upper classes and the munitions factory owners can go on making money from this damned war."

The speaker was short and stocky, broad across the shoulders and had wide, gnarled hands that clenched into fists as he spoke. His uniform was that of an English soldier, but it was oddly neat and well pressed. His face was wrinkled and world-weary even though he looked no more than twenty-five or -six, but his voice overflowed with passion and his body jerked when he spoke, as if electricity were passing through it.

"The Russians have been shooting their officers and going home all summer. Now the French are doing the same."

"How d'you know? I ain't heard nothin' 'bout them Frenchies stoppin' fightin'," a man shouted.

It was Sunday afternoon, the only time we had to ourselves. About thirty Canadians and Australians were gathered outside a tent listening to the short man rant on. I hadn't wanted to hear him, but it was my tent and I had got caught up in the crowd on my way to lie down and rest.

"You've not heard because the High Command's keeping it a secret from you. Three French comrades told me that most of their army mutinied this past summer. They refused to fight, some shot their officers and one regiment even marched on Paris. They didn't make it, though. The cavalry was sent in against them. My sources said that one in every ten men in the regiment was picked by lot and shot."

I listened open-mouthed. Frenchmen shooting Frenchmen! It had to be a lie. I couldn't imagine French cavalry battling their own troops, or a regiment standing on parade while every tenth man was selected for execution.

"That's why we're being slaughtered at Ypres," the man went on. "As long as the Germans are busy killing us, they won't realize that the French army's good for nothing and that the kaiser could walk into Paris if he wanted. We should follow the Russian example, shoot a few officers and end the war. Then we can all go home."

I was horrified to hear a murmur of agreement run through the crowd. Who was this lying, foul-mouthed man who was suggesting rebellion, murder and desertion? Ken was an officer. The idea that this man wanted to shoot him made me furious. I pushed forward.

"Who do you think you are?" I shouted. "You're afraid to fight. You'd let the Germans win. You're not even a Canadian. You're just some stinking, lying coward. I bet you've never even been in battle."

I stopped ranting, suddenly scared that the rough man was going to hit me. He didn't. Instead, his coarse face broke into a broad smile and he laughed.

"Quite the little patriotic firebrand," he said. "I didn't think there were any of you left."

A few of the men laughed and I became conscious that everyone was looking at me. I tried to push past the man into my tent but he placed a strong hand on my chest and stopped me.

"Now hold up. You accused me of a lot of things. Some are true and some aren't, but I should have a chance to answer, shouldn't I?"

I nodded reluctantly.

"First, let me introduce myself. The name's Harry Sommerfield." He held out a hand. I ignored it, but stayed where I was.

Sommerfield shrugged and continued. "It's true I wasn't born in Canada, but I went over there in '06 and that makes me as Canadian as most of the boys here." There were nods from some in the crowd.

"As for being afraid to fight, of course I am. *Any* sane man would be, the instant he got a glimpse of what this war is really like." Again nods from some of the older soldiers in the crowd.

"I don't want the Germans to win and I don't think they will. The German boys on the other side of no man's land are just as scared and tired as we are. If we go home, I believe they will, too. And even if I'm wrong, the Germans winning would be better than what we have now — a huge, insatiable meat grinder that's been running for three years, sucking in millions of young men and spitting out corpses. Or the shadows of men so broken in body and mind that they will never be the same again."

Now I was confused. Harry Sommerfield talked calmly and rationally and, even though I violently disagreed with what he was saying, his eyes held me — like a helpless mouse mesmerized by a snake. "Now, as to the more personal accusations." Sommerfied's smile broadened. "I admit that I do stink somewhat — " a few men laughed " — but no more than most and less than a lot, I dare say. But a short while back you also called me a coward. Now that's a serious thing.

"I've seen 'brave' men with chests full of medals reduced to gibbering wrecks by days of shelling or the sight of their best friend's brains smeared along the wall of a trench. Are *they* cowards?"

I stayed silent.

"Of course they're not. They've just been pushed beyond what any sane man can stand.

"I've been down the coal mines at Cumberland and Extension on Vancouver Island, where it's so gassy that a careless spark can create a wall of fire that'll incinerate fifty men before they even have a chance to run. By the Somme River I've seen sixteen-year-old boys walk forward until machine-gun bullets stitched a neat line of holes across their chests. I've heard wounded men in no man's land scream insanely for two days before they died. I've seen men drown in mud holes at Arras when six of their friends weren't strong enough to pull them out. I've felt the last breath of a young German soldier on my cheek while I struggled to pull my bayonet out of his chest." Sommerfield paused for a long minute, still holding me with his stare. Around us the other men stood in a silence I had only ever heard in church. Eventually, Sommerfield continued.

"I've felt fear so intense that I was paralyzed and I've wept uncontrollably at some of the things I've seen and done, but have I run away? No. After every horror I buried my comrades, picked up my rifle and fought on like a good soldier. So, yes, I am a coward. I'm a coward because through all of that I went on doing what the stupid generals wanted. I never stood up and said, 'No!' I never screamed, 'Enough!' I never shot the officer who ordered another thousand young men to go over the top, knowing that half of them would be dead an hour later."

Confusion overwhelmed me now. What was this man talking about? His list of horrors had nothing to do with bravery, honour and fighting for your country. Did it?

Before I could think of anything to say, an Australian in the crowd shouted, "But you did run away, Harry."

Sommerfield turned his stare on the man who had spoken, releasing me.

"Some would say that," he murmured. "Others might say I'm simply fighting a different war. I'm taking as much of a chance coming here as any I took in the front lines. Only difference is, if I'm caught now, it's my own side that'll shoot me, not the Germans."

"You're a deserter," I said with sudden realization.

"That's what some would call me." Sommerfield turned back to look at me. "I've also been called a Socialist, a traitor, a conspirator and a rabble-rouser. I prefer to think of myself as a sheep who has seen the light and no longer wants to be led unprotesting to the slaughterhouse."

Sommerfield gave me his winning smile, but this time it didn't work. My anger had returned with full force. This man *was* a traitor. Whatever he wanted to call it, he had failed in his duty. While courageous men like Ken were sticking it out to the end, he had run off to skulk away from the fighting. What's more, he was trying to persuade other men to follow him. Every time a brave soldier died at the front, Sommerfield and his kind were as much to blame as the Germans. He *would* be shot by his own side if he were caught, but it was no more than he deserved.

"You *are* a traitor!" I yelled, shoving Sommerfield so hard in the chest that he staggered back into the group of men behind him. "You're not a real Canadian. You deserve to be shot."

I forced my way through the crowd into the tent and threw myself down on my cot. Tears of frustration stung my eyes and I balled my fists and beat the bed frame until my knuckles bled. I felt completely alone, away from home and in a dreadful place where I had nothing and no one that I could relate to. I prayed that I would be sent to the Front, where I would be with Ken and life would be a simple matter of fighting Germans.

Chapter 3
The Storm
Etaples, September 1917

I lay on my cot feeling sorry for myself for quite some time. It was hot and I must have drifted off to sleep, because I woke suddenly to the sounds of running feet and yelling outside. I strained to hear what men were shouting, but it was all gibberish as far as I could tell. Gradually I realized that a distant popping sound was gunfire. The Germans are attacking, I thought, sitting bolt upright, but before I could do anything, Bob Macready burst into the tent.

"They shot someone on the bridge into town, McBride," he said, breathlessly. "All hell's breaking loose out there."

"What are you talking about?" I asked. "What do you mean 'shot someone'? Who shot someone?"

Bob's round, cheerful face was flushed and he was gulping air in as fast as he could as he sat on the cot beside mine. He was a new recruit like myself, a farm boy from Saskatchewan with a natural optimism that allowed him to smile through the worst that Etaples could throw at him. He'd told me that his reason for joining up was so that he could travel beyond the boundaries of his father's quarter section. Already, in only a few months, the army had taken him to Calgary, England and France and shown him more of the world than he had ever dreamed of seeing.

"There was a Scottish corporal on the bridge meeting his girl," Bob hurried on. "That Red Cap that everyone hates, Reeve, comes along and tells the soldier that talking to women is not allowed and orders him to move along. No one seems to know exactly what happened, but there was a fight and Reeve shot the man dead.

"The Scots went wild when they heard, and now the Australians and New Zealanders have joined them. Hundreds of men are storming over the bridge into Etaples and tearing up the town. The rest are hunting Red Caps all over the camp. When they find them they beat them and throw them off the bridge into the river."

I could hardly credit what Bob was telling me. Was this the beginning of revolution and mutiny that Sommerfield had said were sweeping through the Russian and French armies?

"It's . . . it's mutiny," I said.

"I reckon it is," Bob agreed.

"What should we do?"

"Anything we like," Bob said with an ironic smile. "There's no one to stop us. The Red Caps are all beat up or hiding and the officers have run away."

"That's what we *can* do," I said, slightly annoyed at Bob's attitude. "What *should* we do?"

"I guess we could go out there and try and find an officer." Bob sounded uncertain and I must admit the thought of heading out into the camp if there was a full-blown riot going on didn't appeal, but we had joined the army. It was our duty to find an officer and get orders.

"Right," I said, standing up. "Let's go, then."

The view outside looked ten times worse than I had imagined from the sounds. It reminded me of a picture of Hell in the illustrated Bible we had at home. Dusk was falling and dark clouds were building high in the eastern sky. A couple of buildings — the camp prison and a supply shed, I supposed — were ablaze. Deep red flames leaped into the air.

Men were running everywhere, to no obvious purpose. Many were carrying rifles with bayonets attached and several were firing aimlessly into the sky. Over to my left, a group of obviously drunk men had linked arms and were singing a song whose words were drowned out by the general cacophony. There wasn't an officer in sight.

A man barged around the corner of the tent and cannoned into me, knocking me hard against Bob and almost taking all three of us to the ground.

"Hey!" Bob shouted. "Be careful."

The man laughed. "No time to be careful, mate," he said in a broad Australian accent. "The camp's ours. So's the town. Better 'urry over afore all the women're taken and the drink gone."

I watched him disappear into the mad crowd, thinking that at least it didn't sound as if he was part of a revolution to overthrow the army and end the war.

"Let's go to the bridge and see what's happening there," Bob suggested.

As we pushed our way through the chaos, I noticed that several large groups of men stood still, not taking any part in the upheaval. Others stared nervously out from their tents.

As we neared the bridge, I noticed a group of soldiers surrounding the small wooden guard hut at the near end. They were beating on the walls and door with fists and rifle butts. As I stared, the crowd pulled back and a man with a huge axe stepped forward. He only needed to work on the door for a few minutes before it was reduced to splinters.

He threw the axe down and stepped inside the hut. He emerged moments later dragging a terrified Red Cap. The man had his hands clenched and was obviously pleading for his life. The soldier who had broken down the door ignored his pleas, dragged the man to his feet and punched him in the face, sending a spray of blood from his nose. The Red Cap collapsed and disappeared in a forest of feet and fists as the crowd surged forward.

"We should help him," I said.

I was relieved when Bob grabbed my arm and said, "Don't be crazy. They'll tear us apart. Besides, it's probably too late."

For an instant the side of the crowd closest to us parted and I caught a glimpse of the Red Cap. He was huddled on the ground, his usually smart uniform filthy and torn. His face was a bloody mask and his head jerked spastically as a boot connected with the back of his neck. Then the legs closed in around him again.

I felt nauseous. Yes, the Red Caps were brutes and one of them might have murdered the Scottish soldier on the bridge, but did the man in the guard hut deserve to be beaten to death by a drunken mob? His battered face stayed with me as we worked our way around to one side of the bridge.

"You men. Get over here." An authoritative voice cut through the noise.

I looked over to see a solitary officer down the bank beside the oily water of the inlet. There was a line of about twenty armed soldiers behind him. I felt an immense sense of relief. Here was some sanity in the midst of madness. Someone was here to tell me what to do. Bob and I scrambled down the bank.

"There's some spare rifles at the back," the officer said. "Grab one each and join the line. We're going to clear the bridge."

The effect of the officer's calm orders was immense and Bob and I obeyed him without thought. It was only when we had our weapons and began climbing the bank that the lunacy of what we were trying to do sank in. A disturbance among the crowd on the bridge caught my eye and I turned my head just in time to see the limp body of a Red Cap splash into the shallow water below. I had no idea whether it was the one we had seen beaten earlier, but the sight made me and several others in the line, hesitate.

There were hundreds of men packed onto the bridge, many leaning over and jeering at the body of the Red Cap. They were angry, armed, and a good number of them were drunk. We didn't stand a chance.

28

"Stay together and keep moving," the officer ordered. We obeyed. Surprisingly, despite some jeers and shouts, the men on the bank moved back and allowed us to form our line on the flat ground beside the bridge. The sun had set, but the sky was still light behind the men on the bridge.

"I order you men to disperse," the officer said in a loud, clear voice. He had unholstered his pistol but was holding it by his side. "You will clear the bridge and return to your tents."

For a moment the men hesitated. The habit of obeying orders was strong. They're going to do it, I thought. Then the large man who had wielded the axe against the guard hut stepped forward.

"We ain't goin' nowhere," he roared. Behind him a rumble of agreement ran through the crowd. "We got rid of them damned Red Caps. We can get rid of an officer an' a few of his lily-livered flunkeys."

"This doesn't look good," Bob muttered.

"This is mutiny," the officer replied. "The penalty for mutiny is death."

He turned to face us. "Ready," he said, loudly enough for the crowd to hear. We held our rifles across our chests.

"Aim!" We lifted our weapons to our shoulders and pointed them at the crowd.

I stared along my rifle at the packed mass of men before me. Could I shoot? Could I kill another man? My rifle barrel was shaking and, however hard I tried, I couldn't keep it steady. Then I realized that I hadn't even checked to see if the weapon was loaded.

"Mutiny, is it?" the big man said. "There'll be deaths if you want, right enough. I daresay you'll get a few of us, but the only certain deaths'll be yours. Go ahead, shoot your own men."

Several of the rifle barrels were wavering now.

"Steady," the officer shouted. He slowly raised his pistol and pointed it at the big man. "The only certainty is that your death will be the first."

For what seemed like an age, all possible futures hung in the balance. One wrong step and all hell would break loose, and Bob and I would be very unlikely to survive it. Then Harry Sommerfield pushed his way through the crowd.

"Now, boys," he said almost conversationally. "There's no need for all this talk of death."

The officer hesitated for a moment and then swung his pistol over to cover Sommerfield, who continued talking.

"I'll die. You'll die and, I daresay, several others will, too." Sommerfield looked directly at me and smiled. "And what good will it do? Nothing will change.

"The boys are a little out of control tonight, but who can blame them after what they've had to put up with in this place. You and a couple of dozen scared boys can't stop them. We are in the situation we are, and nothing can change that. We can only look for a way out at the other end, and I have a suggestion that'll save a lot of bloodshed."

The officer was uncertain. His pistol wavered. Sommerfield undoubtedly had charm, but I was confused. This was not the firebrand who had incited the men to revolution earlier.

"All these boys want," Sommerfield went on, "is a chance to have their grievances heard and improve the conditions in this place. They want to be treated like human beings, like men who are fighting for their country, and not donkeys who have to be beaten and degraded by Red Caps whose only contact with Germans was with waiters in London before the war. We want to meet the camp commander and discuss things."

"This is the army," the officer responded, "not one of your damned labour unions. Soldiers obey orders. They don't negotiate and discuss the best thing to do."

"Then there will be bloodshed," Sommerfield said, so softly we had to strain to hear him. He stepped forward, reached out to steady the officer's pistol and aimed it at his face. "Let's get to it."

Beside me, Bob gasped. However grudgingly, I had to admire Sommerfield's courage. He was staring unblinkingly at the officer, and I knew the power of those eyes. Slowly the pistol lowered until it was pointing at the ground. The tension eased.

"I shall arrange a meeting with the general to discuss this matter. Prepare a list of grievances." He turned to face us. "Order arms."

I was almost laughing with relief as I lowered my rifle to my side. The crowd on the bridge was rolling forward, everyone intent on congratulating Sommerfield. The big man who had spoken first grabbed him and, with the help of a couple of others, lifted him up to ride on their shoulders.

"Slope arms," the officer ordered and we placed our rifles on our shoulders. "Left turn. Form column. Forward march."

The mob parted to let us through, although several men jeered as we passed. Behind us I could hear ragged cheering. That night, for the first time in years, my dreams were haunted by the face of the dying deer.

❖   ❖   ❖

Sommerfield got his meeting with the camp commander the next day. He presented a list of demands for greater access to the town, closure of the hated parade ground, removal of the Red Caps and better food and conditions. The general refused.

The mutiny at Etaples dragged on for a week and, although the men continued to control the camp, there was no repeat of the violence of that first night. Eventually the general caved and agreed to all of Sommerfield's demands. It was a victory, but Sommerfield didn't see it. He had slipped quietly away two days before.

I didn't see it either, and only heard about the rest of that week much later. The day after that violent Sunday, Bob and I and hundreds of other men were loaded onto trains and shipped east to Ypres and Passchendaele.

Chapter 4
Disappointment
Outside Cassel, September 1917

"What in *hell* are you doing here, Allan?"

Those were the first words Ken said to me as I walked through the gates of the Canadian camp outside Cassel. The journey from Etaples should have only taken a few hours, but we had spent most of the past three days sitting in railway sidings watching endless lines of troop and ammunitions trains rumble by towards Ypres.

"I've come to fight," I explained, taken aback by the harshness of his tone. I had never even heard Ken swear before.

I had arrived at Cassel, almost as excited as I had been on the train down to Vancouver to sign up. I was glad to get Etaples behind me, eager to be a part of the big battle that was obviously coming, and thrilled to be seeing Ken again. "Didn't you get my letter?" I asked.

"What letter?"

"I wrote you in August from England saying that I had managed to get transferred to your battalion and that I would probably be over in France in a few weeks."

"I never got it. Things go missing here. Oh Christ, Allan, why did you have to come? And now of all times."

I stood in silence, wracked by doubt. One of the things that had got me through the endless, mindless training and the brutality of Etaples had been the thought that soon I would be beside Ken. We would be together just as we had been in the hills above the Nicola Valley, except now we would be united in fighting for a just cause. Now here he was at last, except that he was obviously furious at seeing me. "Well. You're here," he said. "Best go and find your billet. We'll talk later."

That was it. No welcome. No questions about people back home. I think Ken's introduction to Cassel upset me more than everything that had happened at Etaples — and I had plenty of time to dwell on it. For more than two hours we twenty replacement soldiers stood around in the open waiting for the army to get around to assigning us to our new homes.

"That's the army for you," Bob said as we stood at the edge of the parade ground. "Hurry up and wait."

Cassel was 20 miles from Ypres and showed few

signs of the war except for the huge dumps of supplies dotting the surrounding countryside and the vast Canadian camp. The town itself was set on a hill that dominated the surrounding flat plain. At least for this part of the world it was a hill, although back home in British Columbia it wouldn't even be a pimple.

"It's annoying me," Bob said, his brow furrowed.

"What is?"

"The name, Cassel. I know it from somewhere, but I can't for the life of me remember where."

I left Bob to his memories and looked around. The Canadian camp sprawled over the plain at the foot of the hill. Tents and rough wooden huts stretched as far as the eye could see. Groups of soldiers — some ten or twenty men, some several hundred — marched in all directions. Officers and sergeants barked orders and, in the distance, I could hear the *pop* of firing from the rifle range. I felt a surge of pride at being a part of this great Canadian contribution to the war.

"Oh, the Grand Old Duke of York,
He had ten thousand men.
He marched them up to the top of the hill,
And he marched them down again."

For a moment I thought Bob had gone crazy, reciting nursery rhymes, then he smiled and said, "That was Cassel."

"What was?"

"The hill that the Grand Old Duke of York marched up. It was Cassel. That's where I've heard the name before. One of my teachers at school told us where all the old nursery rhymes come from and that was one. More than a hundred years ago, the English army attacked Cassel. They failed; that's why they had to march back down again."

"What's it like being in your mind?" I groaned. "With so much useless information, there can't be any room for anything else."

"You never know when things will come in handy," Bob replied with a laugh.

"Attention!"

We snapped to attention and faced the major who stood before us. A sergeant holding a clipboard stood beside him.

"My name's Major Fraser Carmichael and this is Sergeant Fairley. In a moment he will give you your company and platoon assignments.

"Welcome to the 2nd Division and don't ever forget that you are here to do a job and in doing that job you will be representing the Dominion of Canada. Good luck.

"Carry on, Sergeant."

Major Carmichael saluted, turned and strode away.

"A man of few words," Bob said out of the side of his mouth.

"All right, you lot, listen up," the sergeant's voice boomed out. "When you're dismissed, you will collect your kit and go straight to the Company billet. That will be your world from now on. You will stow your kit sharpish and report to the parade ground."

The sergeant read out all our names and our company and platoon assignments. Bob and I were both in 2 Platoon of B Company — Ken's Company.

"Private McBride. Report immediately to Captain Harrison in the Company command tent."

The sergeant barked the order from the door of the billet and I knew enough of the army by then to jump to my feet, button my tunic and hurry outside. Bob and I had spent the afternoon marching back and forth, just as we had at Etaples, but with the difference that there were no hated Red Caps and no one talked of mutiny and revolution. In fact, there was a quiet confidence in the soldiers I talked to. Everyone knew that there would be casualties, probably very heavy ones, in the coming battle, but the entire Canadian Corps would be fighting together under a Canadian commander. We were proud. At B Company command tent, the sergeant announced me and stepped aside. I ducked in, stood at attention and saluted. Ken was sitting on a camp stool behind a folding desk, concentrating on a pile of forms. There was a half-empty bottle of whiskey and a glass beside him. It was dusk already and a gas lantern hissed in the corner. Ken finished writing something and looked up. He seemed weary and older than I remembered him.

"At ease, Allan," he said. "This isn't formal army business. I wanted to apologize for being so brusque earlier. It was a shock to see you. I thought you were safe at home."

"I had to come and do my bit," I said.

Ken tried to smile. "I suppose you did. Anyway, you're here now, so we must make the best of it. I intend to request that you be transferred to the Canadian 5th Division. They are still forming and training in England. The request will take some time, but we have that. The 2nd Division is not scheduled to take part in the first phase of the upcoming battle. That honour has been allotted the 3rd and 4th Divisions. We will be held in reserve until needed. Meanwhile, I shall assign you duties around the camp. It will be dull, but it will keep you out of harm's way." He paused and stared at me.

Slowly the meaning of what Ken was saying sank in. He intended to shuffle me off to some new unit that wasn't even in France yet.

"No," I said. "I told you that I've come to do my bit and I intend to. I specifically requested that I be assigned to your unit. I've been through months of training and travel to get here. I've been through the riots at Etaples. I did all this just so I could get here and fight beside you. We'll be together just like when we were hunting and fishing before the war. You can't send me away. If you do transfer me out I'll simply request a transfer back. If you don't want me in your Company, I'll ask to go to any other unit that is going into action."

I hadn't meant to launch into such a rant, but everything just burst out. Through all the endless marching and drilling in Calgary and England, the confusing harshness of Etaples, and the struggle to learn that I was no longer an individual with the power to think, but a tiny, mindless unit in a huge machine — through all that — I had kept going because every step took me closer to fighting at Ken's side. Now he was sending me away. I wasn't going to let him.

Ken tilted his head to one side and regarded me thoughtfully for a long time. When he eventually spoke, his voice was so quiet that I found myself leaning forward to catch what he was saying. "I suppose it's my fault for not telling you what this damned war was really like, but then I don't know if it's even possible to tell someone who hasn't been through it."

I started to say that it wasn't Ken's fault, that I had made my own decision, but he held up his hand to silence me.

"Do you remember how enthusiastic I was when I volunteered back in 1914? God, it seems like an eternity ago. I remember being glad that the war had stalled so I would get my chance. I hadn't even arrived at the war yet, but when the Germans used poison gas at Ypres in 1915, it only proved to me what monsters we were fighting against. All that changed one day just before I came home for that Christmas of 1916." Ken poured some whiskey into his glass and took a drink before beginning his story.

"It was the tail end of the Somme battle and we'd been trying for days to take this German strongpoint. It was cold and rainy and the mud was dreadful. It seemed like every day the artillery would open up in the morning, we'd charge forward, only to find that the German wire hadn't been cut. We'd try and find a way through while the machine guns shot us down, and then those who were still alive would struggle back, collect some reserves and try again the next day.

"One day a young piper from the unit beside mine played his men forward. When they reached the uncut wire he stood up straight and walked back and forth playing a strathspey reel. It was the bravest act I've ever seen. He was just a kid, with red hair. He stumbled a few times in the mud, but not a bullet touched him. It was a miracle if ever I've seen one. His courage inspired the men so much that they rushed the wire, broke through and stormed the strongpoint." Ken lowered his head and massaged his temples with his fingers, his eyes tight shut. Eventually, he lifted his head and continued. "I met the piper later that day in no man's land. He'd taken a wounded man back — that was a piper's job after an attack — and was returning to collect his pipes. I stopped him and said how impressed I had been by his courage. 'It were nothin', sir,' he said. 'It's ma job.' He made light of it, but I could see from the faint smile that played round his mouth that he was proud and that my compliment had meant something to him. Then we parted."

Ken again stopped telling me the story and rubbed his eyes. When he did continue, his voice was little more than a hoarse whisper and I had to lean over his desk to hear him.

"I heard the shell coming and threw myself down. I don't know whether the piper didn't hear the shell or hadn't been out long enough to recognize when one was coming at you. In any case he kept walking. I yelled at him to get down, but he didn't hear me.

"The shell must have exploded no more than a couple of feet from him. I had buried my face in the mud and felt the blast wash over me. When I looked up, the boy was gone, at least most of him was. His legs were still there, lying on the lip of the crater the explosion had made, but there was nothing above the waist." Ken lifted his glass with a shaking hand and drained it.

"I must have been in shock, because I remember thinking that I had to help him. I reached over to push myself up and felt something. The boy's head, still attached to his right arm and shoulder, was lying right beside me. A piece of the shell must have torn that part of him away from his chest. It was a hideous, grisly mess, but his face was completely untouched, exactly as it had been a moment before when I was speaking to him. His eyes were open and the smile was still on his lips. For a moment I stared at him, waiting for him to say, 'It's nothin', sir.' Then I screamed."

I was horrified by what Ken was telling me, as much by his increasingly haggard look as by the story of the young piper.

"I don't remember a lot about the days after that. Apparently I staggered into the Company command post talking gibberish. They sent me back to the casualty clearing station, where I was lucky to be seen by a doctor who realized that I was in shock. Somehow he managed to get me onto the leave roster and that's how I came home for Christmas.

"It was a struggle to hide how I felt. The nightmares were bad and my hands would suddenly shake for no reason. But being in the Valley and seeing that you were safe helped. I figured that, whatever I had to go through, at least you would be all right.

"When I came back, I heard that they'd made me captain. Since then I've got by as best I can, and I've been lucky. We were part of the reserves at Vimy — "

"But Vimy Ridge was a great Canadian victory," I interrupted. "How can you think yourself lucky to have missed it?"

"Oh it was a great victory all right," Ken said, his voice heavy with sarcasm. "In four days, we had three and a half thousand men killed and another seven thousand shattered in body and mind to take a hill that you and I would have walked over in half an hour when we were deer hunting. We should all be proud — except maybe that Canadian soldier who deserted back in February and told the Germans we were coming."

I recoiled at the anger and bitterness in Ken's voice. He was so different from the friend I had known back home. Before I could think of anything to say, he continued.

"I haven't been in battle since the Somme, but that doesn't stop the nightmares. They come and go, as they do for most men who have been out here for any length of time. But the shaking has stopped and the whiskey helps a little."

Ken nodded at the bottle on the table. He gave me a half-smile and shrugged apologetically. "I'm not the hero you imagine. There are no heroes out here, just the living and the dead. Let me put you up for that transfer to the 5th Division."

I stood in silence for a long time, absorbing what Ken had told me. Was this tired cynic who hid from his nightmares in a whiskey bottle the friend I had admired more than anyone else? Could the war change someone *this* much? I was certain of one thing — it wasn't going to change me.

"I don't want a transfer to somewhere safe," I said. "I came here to do my bit and I mean to do it. I know horrible things happen in war. I'm ready for it."

Ken's face slumped and he closed his eyes and sighed. "Very well," he said. "If that's what you wish."

I stood to attention and saluted. As I turned to leave, Ken said, "One moment." I turned back. He was looking up at me.

"Do you still remember that deer you shot years ago?"

I nodded.

"I never understood what you meant when you talked about the nightmares you had afterwards. I thought you were just a kid who would grow out of it, but you never did, did you?"

"No."

"I just want to let you know that I understand now. That's all."

Ken picked up the whiskey bottle and poured a large measure into his glass. I had no idea what to say. I saluted once more and left the tent.

I trudged back to my billet, deep in thought. I suppose I had always known on some level that the war would not be what I had expected when I was sitting in my bedroom back home reading the newspapers, but the revolutionary talk of Harry Sommerfield, the riot at Etaples and Ken's collapse — what could I make of all that? Sommerfield I could dismiss as a radical crank, simply out to make trouble. And the riots did have a cause in the brutal conditions the men were under. But Ken's despondency was a huge shock. He had been the one certainty I had clung to despite everything else.

That was my first clue that war wasn't simply a question of fighting and surviving or not. War had the power to change people in frightening ways and, if it could change Ken, it might change me, too. I felt suddenly cast adrift.

"*There* you are."

I looked up to see Bob approaching. The broad smile on his face was a welcome sight. "Now that you've been released by the high and mighty, it's time to descend to reality. We've drawn guard duty."

I hurried back to collect my rifle and followed Bob to the guardhouse to receive our instructions.

Chapter 5
The Sound of the Guns
Ypres, November 4, 1917

The recent rain made the rounded tops of the cobblestones so slick that the metal studs on my boots kept slipping to the side, making it difficult to keep in step with the rest of my platoon. Everyone was having difficulty and the rhythmic sound of marching feet was punctuated by the occasional curse. We had been singing for much of the 20 miles from Cassel, but that had stopped as soon as we reached the outskirts of what was left of Ypres.

Years of shelling had reduced the town to rubble. Piles of grey bricks were often all that marked the site of a large building. Here and there, solitary, shell-pitted walls stood, their glassless windows like blank, staring eyes. In some places the building had been destroyed so long ago that grass and weeds grew thickly over the rubble.

The dull thud of distant artillery sounded from so many directions that it seemed as if we were walking into the mouth of some vast cannon.

Dark, heavy clouds, hanging so low that I felt I could almost reach up and touch them, weighed down on us and perfectly matched our mood as we slogged through the rubble. Ypres was my first glimpse of the world of war.

Through the latter half of September and the beginning of October, while the Canadian divisions had been gathering and training around Cassel, the British, Australians and New Zealanders had been fighting in the mud and rain at Polygon Wood, Poelcappelle, along the Menin Road and outside the village of Passchendaele. Casualties had been high and I wondered how many of them had been men that I had seen rioting at Etaples.

Despite the rain, the mud and the casualties, the Front had been edging nearer to Passchendaele. At the end of October, the 3rd and 4th Canadian Divisions pushed even closer. Now it was our turn to relieve them and secure the village before winter set in properly. I was excited and terrified in equal measure.

"Chance of a lifetime," Bob said, looking at two scarred walls — all that was left of what must once have been a large house. "Desirable open-plan property with uninterrupted views in all directions. Owner motivated to sell."

I laughed. It never ceased to amaze me how,

regardless of what misery we were experiencing, Bob always managed to retain his sense of humour.

"Needs a little work," I said.

"Nothing a young man with a good strong back couldn't handle. Besides, you want it open so you can hear the shells coming."

I laughed again. Bob and I had grown close since my meeting with Ken. It seemed that his cheerful outlook and ready smile were the things I remembered from my childhood with Ken, and which were missing from him now. I saw Ken a lot during our training and we had even talked a few times, but there was a distance between us that was more than that between a company commander and a private. At least he had honoured my request and not put my name forward for a transfer.

"Did you see the Old Bill cartoon in the army paper the other day?" Bob asked.

"No."

"It showed two old men with white beards sitting in a trench with hundreds of shells whistling overhead. One of them's reading a paper. The caption says, *A.D. Nineteen Fifty, 'I see the War Babies Battalion is coming out.'*"

"That's not funny," I said. "Some people have been saying that the war might last that long."

"Nonsense," Bob shot back. "The Americans are in it now. As soon as enough of them get over here we'll end this thing."

"But the Russians look like they're finished," I pointed out, "so it all balances. I heard a couple of men talking the other day about this new tactic of 'bite and hold' that the generals have come up with."

"It makes sense to me," Bob said. "The big breakthrough wasn't happening, so why not aim for smaller objectives? Besides, it's working. We've pushed the German lines back quite a bit in the past few weeks."

"That's what those men were talking about," I said. "One of them had worked out that, at the rate we're advancing now with this 'bite and hold' plan, we'll get to Berlin in three hundred years."

That silenced Bob and, as the first drops of rain fell, we plodded on.

We struggled forward in the rain all through the night of November 4, sometimes stopping to rest or allow other parties past, but always moving closer to the thunder and bright flashes of the guns. Once we sat for a few minutes close to one of our guns, a squat ugly thing with gunners moving around it like black ghosts. When the gun fired, it was like being in the centre of a thunderstorm. The noise was like a physical blow, battering my head and dulling my senses, and leaving my ears ringing for a full hour afterwards. The flash lit up the stark, devastated landscape with an unnatural brightness, making the splintered tree look like the broken fingers of ancient buried giants.

As we approached the front lines, the mud became worse and we stumbled and slipped along wooden duckboards. When we slipped off, our boots sank up to our ankles and it was the devil's own job to pull our feet out. The mud seemed to be an evil, living presence, determined to draw us down into the depths. I was reminded of Sommerfield's story of some men being sucked down and drowning in mud holes because their comrades didn't have the strength to pull them free.

It got even worse when Ken and Sergeant Fairley ordered us into the communications trench that led to the front line. Whenever we slipped here, we fell against the trench walls and were soon completely covered in a layer of heavy, disgusting, slimy clay. We were frozen, filthy, wet and exhausted by the time we reached our goal and Ken quietly told us to stand easy. He moved a heavy gas curtain aside from the door of a half-buried machine-gun pillbox and disappeared inside to confer with the officer of the Company we were relieving.

Despite my tiredness, my excitement remained. This was the front line, the battle zone. The enemy that my country had been fighting for more than three years was standing in a similar hole in the ground only a couple of hundred yards away. I looked around, trying to take in as much as possible by the dim light of a few small cooking fires and the occasional harsh brightness of the flares that burst overhead.

My first impression was of being in a dump. Pieces of equipment, torn sandbags and garbage were everywhere. The smell was overpowering — the sharp odour of gunpowder, a pervasive outhouse stink, and the lingering smell of gas that I recognized from training. Beneath it all was another smell that I couldn't identify — unpleasant, but strangely sweet.

All around I could hear the distant *crump* of artillery, ours and the Germans', but none of the shells was landing close. Clusters of rifle shots popped now and then and the rhythmic *clack* of machine guns burst out from time to time. The flares that lit up the scene added a soft hissing sound to the music of war.

The trench was little more than a deep winding ditch. The floor was covered with duckboards like the ones we had been struggling over for hours. The walls were mud, supported here and there by sandbags, which in places had slumped down. The trench was mostly about 6 feet deep, but in some places was less than 4. In spots it was so narrow that two men could barely pass. In others it spread a good 10 feet wide where a shell had exploded. By the light of the flares I could see about 20 feet in either direction before the trench bent away. It was nothing like the neat trenches we had trained in. There everything had been regular and the trench walls — parapet to the front, parados to the back — were solid and secure. From above, the training trenches looked like the battlements of a medieval castle laid out on the ground. Ours must have looked like a twisted line of knotted yarn.

Two men stood, 10 feet apart, on overturned ammunition boxes, peering out into the night. Others moved back and forth along the trench carrying mortars, ammunition, sandbags and shovels. A corporal and three men to my right were busy repairing a place where the trench wall had partially collapsed. While I watched, the corporal stepped back with a curse as a section of the wall slumped down in front of him. I stared as the mudslide revealed a decomposed human body. What was left of the torso was held together by the rags of a uniform, but the head — little more than a grinning skull — detached and bounced into the bottom of the trench. A strong stench of the same sweet smell I had noticed earlier made me cover my mouth and nose.

"Dammit," the corporal said, "that's why the wall collapsed. Bodies don't hold together once they start to rot."

He bent and picked up the skull and tossed it over the edge of the trench. Then he looked up at me and laughed.

"New boy, eh?" he asked. "You'll get used to it. Besides — " he turned and drove his shovel into the body's chest " — it's only a Gerry.

"Come on, you lot," he shouted at the other three men who had stopped work when the body appeared, "We ain't got all night. Put your backs into it. The sooner we get this brave young man of the kaiser's army out of the trench, the sooner the smell'll improve and the sooner we can get the parapet built up proper."

The men began swinging their shovels and cutting the body up. I heard the sound of someone retching, but my attention was pulled away by Ken coming out of the pillbox. He conferred briefly with the lieutenants who commanded the four platoons and the information was passed on to the sergeants and corporals who commanded each section. My section of twelve men under Sergeant MacTaggart was assigned to the stretch of trench I was standing in.

For the next hour there was a lot of back and forth as we settled in and the previous occupants departed. My new home was a typical funk-hole — 4 feet long, 2 feet high, scooped out from the wall of the trench and just deep enough for me to curl into. I could never stretch out and it was always wet, but it kept the worst of the rain off.

Bob had the funk-hole next to mine. He called his the Savoy Hotel, but we had no chance to use them.

"Stand to," Sergeant MacTaggart ordered as dawn began to lighten the sky above the German trenches. We hurriedly unwrapped the canvas covers that had kept the mud out of our rifles, and mounted the fire-step. I got my first glimpse of no man's land.

Of course none of the enemy was in sight. One of the extraordinary things about the battlefields around Ypres was that you could look over a land-scape containing thousands of soldiers and not see a single one. To stand up in the open here was to invite a sniper's bullet or a burst of machine-gun fire.

The view as the sun rose was like nothing I could have imagined. It was like the surface of some alien planet. The dead trunks of trees, stripped of every leaf and branch by shellfire, were the only things standing above the tortured ground. Here and there, twisted piles of barbed wire and rusting sheets of torn corrugated iron lay like toys discarded by huge, petulant children.

So many explosions had happened here that it was not even possible to distinguish individual shell holes. Scattered paler patches showed the sites of ruined pillboxes, and redder piles of rubble where farmhouses used to be. How could this ever have been a scene of cows grazing on green fields? We gazed in silence at the devastation. Even Bob didn't have a humorous comment.

"See yon patch of reddish ground right in front of us?" MacTaggart said in his broad Scottish accent. "That's the village of Passchendaele."

I had known that any village this close to the front lines would be severely damaged, and I had seen what shelling had done to Ypres, but Passchendaele had literally ceased to exist. Barely one brick sat atop another.

"See, yon building?" MacTaggart asked.

I stared hard at where he was pointing and could just make out a pile of rubble about the height of a man.

"I admit there's not much left of it," MacTaggart went on, "but it used to be a church. Take a good look. That's the centre of Passchendaele and that's where we'll be headed tomorrow morning."

I tried to imagine how it would be possible to get from where I was now over to the ruined church, even without the German army trying to stop me. I couldn't do it.

Over to my right a machine gun clattered. In response, I heard our guns firing behind me. Small, almost beautiful, puffs of black and white smoke blossomed above the wasteland.

"The morning hate," MacTaggart informed us. "Best get yer heads down now. Gerry knows that something's up so he'll be sending a few of his own over afore long. Not to mention that I also heard that there's a Gerry sniper working from the ruined pillboxes in no man's land."

We ducked down into the trench and, sure enough, almost immediately we heard the whistle of shells arriving, followed by the *crump* of explosions. None came particularly close to us, and MacTaggart told us newcomers what each sound meant and what to do.

"That long drawn-out whine, yon's a big gun, high explosive. If the whine keeps getting louder, get yerself down, hug the dirt and pray. Nothing else to be done.

"That higher pitch, yon's a shrapnel shell. Explodes above the ground and no problem if yer in the trench unless it explodes directly overhead. The real bad ones are the trench mortars — Minnies, we call them. They make a sort of coughing sound when they're fired and they're the very devil to hear coming. But we won't have to worry about them here. Gerry trenches are too far away.

"Now, get yer rifles cleaned and brew up tea. We've got a lot of housekeeping to do. Those boys from the 4th Division have left this place a pigsty, but they're mostly from Manitoba, so what can ye expect.

"McBride, you get yerself down the sap yonder and keep yer ears open and yer eyes peeled. You'll be relieved in two hours. And don't forget the sniper. Keep yer head down."

"Yes, Sergeant." I grabbed my rifle and headed down the sap.

❖   ❖   ❖

The sap was in an even worse state than the trench, little more than a ditch running out into no man's land and ending in a shallow hole not even deep enough to stand upright in. I settled in as best I could and peered through the wooden periscope that stuck up above the lip of the sap and gave me a narrow view of no man's land. I tried not to think how lonely and exposed I was out in front of the lines, but at least it was daylight and I had a chance of seeing any attack coming. At night, every shadow is an approaching enemy and every sound the pin being pulled from a grenade.

During my two hours of shivering duty, I forced myself to remember that I was the eyes and ears of the army and that I could be shot for falling asleep. Nevertheless, my eyes were drooping when I heard someone working their way along the sap towards me, I assumed it was my replacement, but I was wrong.

"Well, you've got your wish," Ken said as he squeezed in beside me. "We go into battle tomorrow."

"I know," I replied.

"I don't suppose it'll do any good, but I have to designate ten per cent of the Company to stay behind. Will you let me put your name on the list?"

"No," I said, although after looking at where we had to go, there was a part of me that wanted to say yes.

"I thought not. All I can do then is wish you good luck."

"Thanks, and you. Why do you have to select ten per cent of the Company?"

Ken shrugged. "So there will be a core of the old Company to build around if none of us come back tomorrow."

A chill ran down my spine. Was that really possible?

"What the men usually do," Ken went on, "is write a letter and give it to one of those left behind to be mailed if they don't come back." Ken looked hard at me. I couldn't think of anything to say.

"Back in September," he went on eventually, "you said you had been in Etaples during the riots."

I nodded.

"What exactly happened?"

Ken listened intently as I gave him a brief description of what I had seen.

"Who was the man who gave the political speeches?" he asked when I had finished.

"He said his name was Harry Sommerfield. Why, do you know him?"

"Not personally, but there are stories about him — little more than rumours, really. Apparently he was a coal miner and union activist on Vancouver Island. He led strikes and made a lot of enemies

61

among the mine owners. God alone knows why a man like that would join the army, but he did. Served on the Somme, but disappeared late in 1916. Story is that he leads a mixed band of deserters north of here in the woods by the Yser River. The army's sent patrols on sweeps through the area but never caught anyone but a few stragglers."

"He's a powerful man," I said, remembering Sommerfield's eyes and how they held me.

"So I've heard," Ken agreed. "He seems to have no trouble convincing men that his ideas are right. Some of the wilder elements in the army look on him as a sort of folk hero, a man who would stop the war if he had the power."

"A *hero?* Sommerfield?" I asked.

"Not everyone is as keen to go into battle as you, Allan. This war wears men down, even when they're not fighting. There's a story going around that the end of the war will be announced by the firing of a black flare at midnight, but of course no one will see it. There are soldiers here who have been in this war almost their entire adult lives. They can barely imagine anything else, let alone see the war ever end. Not even the generals talk of breakthroughs any more. It's just a war of attrition, a slogging match that will go on until every soldier is dead or crippled or insane.

"Add to that the revolutions in Russia and the mutinies in the French army, and the news that the Italians have collapsed at Caporetto and may soon be out of the war, and it's not difficult to see how pessimism can grow and how a man like Sommerfield can become powerful."

I groaned at more of Ken's misery and cynicism, but something he said intrigued me. "Will there be a revolution here?"

"No," Ken said, "although I sometimes wish there would be. Something has to change. But from what you told me about Etaples, despite Harry Sommerfield, the men who were rioting were simply fed up with the harsh conditions. In the short term, they just wanted to get drunk and find some excitement in town, and in the long term they just wanted better treatment. As far as I know, not a single man from Etaples refused to go to the Front when he was called."

We sat in silence for a while as I scanned no man's land through the periscope. I was getting better at recognizing features and could make out the ruined concrete pillboxes where MacTaggart had said a sniper was hiding. They looked completely deserted to me.

"Fishing in the Valley was a long time ago. A different world."

The strangely wistful tone in Ken's voice made me take my eye from the periscope. He was sitting with his back against the sap wall, staring up at the grey sky.

"The sky there was so blue. Sometimes I wonder if such a place even exists anymore, or if the entire world is grey mud and death."

"Of course it exists," I said. "You saw it yourself last Christmas and I left it only a few months ago. We'll go back to it when this is all over."

Ken lowered his gaze and looked at me. "If you say so," he whispered. Then he closed his eyes briefly, took a deep breath and added, "But there's work to do before then."

At that moment, my relief came round the corner in the sap. He was a new recruit, awkward, nervous and, if anything, even younger than me. I think his name was Peter, but everyone called him Lofty because he was so tall and skinny. At the sight of an officer, he automatically straightened up and saluted.

The sniper's bullet caught him in the left temple and blew a ragged hole in the back of his helmet. Lofty looked surprised and sat down. By the time I reached him, he was blinking stupidly. As I undid his helmet strap, I heard Ken say softly, "No."

The helmet came away and with it a large

piece of the boy's skull, large gouts of blood and some pieces of grey matter. Lofty sighed almost gratefully and his eyes closed. I retched onto the sap floor.

When I was done, I looked over at Ken. He was staring wide-eyed and unblinking at the body.

"Ken, what should we do?" I asked, but got no response.

I leaned over and shook Ken's shoulder. "Sir," I said more formally. "What are your orders?"

Ken seemed to drag himself back from some far-away place. He blinked and turned to look at me.

"Orders. Yes, of course," he said. "Stay here on guard. I'll get another relief and someone to remove the body."

"Yes, sir," I said as Ken worked his way past Lofty and down the sap. I concentrated on search-ing no man's land through the periscope until Bob and Sergeant MacTaggart arrived to relieve me. Bob and I exchanged places without a word and the sergeant and I dragged the body through the front-line trench and into the communica-tions trench, where we laid it out in a funk-hole to await transport to the rear.

"You all right?" MacTaggart asked when we were done.

"I think so," I said.

"Good. Keep yerself busy and try not to think. It was his own fault."

I tried to take MacTaggart's advice and kept busy at trench repairs and bringing up supplies. Mostly it worked, but when I lay down for a rest that afternoon the dream of the deer returned, only now Lofty's surprised face was there as well. I woke up soaked in sweat more than rain.

Chapter 6
Attack
Passchendaele, November 6, 1917

There was no sleep for anyone that night. Patrols were sent out into no man's land to lay strips of tape over the mud for us to follow in the attack the next morning. Climbing ladders were brought up so that we could get out of the trench rapidly, and reinforcements piled in until there was barely room to move in the front line.

At 0530 hours our guns opened up. It was still night but the streaks of shells above us and the constant flares lit everything up as bright as day. It was like some hellish fireworks celebration.

The roar of the explosions, combined with the whine of the heavy shells passing overhead, was deafening. The ground shook and pieces of the trench wall kept falling in. But it was comforting to know that the Germans were having a much worse time of it than we were. Of course the German guns, those that were left, replied, but it was mostly counter-battery fire aimed at silencing our artillery. It didn't work.

The plan was for a short, very intense bombardment of the German trenches. While this was going on, we would advance as close as we could over no man's land so that when the barrage stopped we could rush in before the Germans could get organized. The barrage would then move on to the German second line and the process would be repeated. For the plan to work, we had to stay close to the falling shells and keep up with the creeping barrage. Timing was everything.

Just before 0600 hours we clambered out of the trenches and edged forward. Sergeant MacTaggart led our section, screaming to be heard above the noise. I couldn't see Ken, but then I couldn't see much through the smoke of the exploding shells.

After only a few yards, I was almost deaf and nearly exhausted. My clothes were soaked through and heavy. Every step sank me deeper into clinging mud, but the mindless thrill of the moment kept me going. Eventually MacTaggart signalled for us to lie down.

The barrage was forming a wall of flame and black smoke terrifyingly near. The ground shook beneath us and clumps of mud landed all around. Then it stopped and an eerie, unbelievable silence descended.

MacTaggart stood up. "Come on, you lazy sods. You can't let the artillery do all the work."

Almost in slow motion we struggled to our feet and trudged forward. I noticed a cluster of twisted bodies to my right where one of our own shells had fallen short.

Our artillery opened up again, but now the wall of explosions was farther away.

"Come on!" MacTaggart shouted.

We crossed the German front-line trenches with ease. They were even less continuous than ours and were little more than a line of shell holes marked by half-buried bodies. If anyone had survived that barrage, they had now fled.

Some of the bodies were torn into pieces and horribly mutilated, but the sight didn't bother me. I felt no emotion whatever. In contrast, I was unnaturally aware of what was going on around me, but in a detached way. I saw men nearby drop and realized that they had been shot, but I felt no fear or sense of danger. Bob was in the same state as me.

"That was easy," he shouted after we crossed the German line. Then the machine gun opened up.

My first thought was that the loud clacking noise was a sewing machine, but then men began to fall all round.

"Get down," MacTaggart yelled before his legs

buckled and he fell into a shell hole. Bob and I dove in after him.

The hole was big enough that we could lie along the side with our heads below the rim and still not be in the pool of foul water in the bottom. MacTaggart was on the far side, clutching his right thigh and swearing profusely.

"Are you hit?" I shouted across.

"Don't be bloody stupid," he replied. "Of course I'm hit."

I crawled around to have a look. The bullet had torn his trousers open midway between his hip and his knee. There was a lot of blood but I couldn't see any bone.

"I think it missed the bone," I said.

"Aye," MacTaggart agreed, "but I'll no be running any races for a while."

"Or chasing any women," Bob muttered.

I cleaned the wound as best I could and put a field dressing on to stop the bleeding.

"What's going on out there?" MacTaggart asked.

Bob crawled over, edged up the side of the hole and peered cautiously over the lip. The sun still wasn't up yet, but the exploding shells and flares bathed the battlefield in an eerie light. "Looks like everybody's taken cover," he said. "The machine gun's got us pinned down. I think I see it, though."

I crawled round to join Bob. The barrage was still going on, but it was farther off now. I felt lonely without it. I could hear other machine guns clatter farther away. It looked as if our whole force was pinned down.

Here and there, helmets popped up from shell holes. If the German gunners spotted them, a spray of bullets made the heads disappear quickly.

"The machine gun's over in that ruined pill-box." Bob pointed at a filthy block of concrete. "Keep looking in that dark hole."

I did as I was told and soon spotted a suggestion of movement.

"I think you're right. I'll take a shot at it."

I worked the bolt on my rifle, steadied it on the lip of the shell hole and aimed for the centre of the dark area. A puff of dust above the hole told me I was too high.

I was busy aiming again when Bob grabbed my jacket and dragged me down just as a line of bullets kicked up clods of dirt all along the lip.

"They've spotted you now," he said. "We'll need to try something else. Look, go over to that side of the hole, as far as you can, and when I give the word, keep down but push your helmet and rifle over the lip."

Again I did as I was told, assuming that Bob was going to take a shot.

"Okay," Bob said.

Cautiously, I took off my helmet and pushed the front edge up. At the same time, I raised the rifle. A burst of machine-gun fire knocked my helmet into the bottom of the shell hole and sent a cascade of dirt over me.

To my amazement, Bob leaped out of the shell hole and disappeared. The line of bullets followed him.

"Are you okay?" I yelled when the firing stopped.

"Yeah," he replied. "I think I can work my way close enough to lob a grenade into the pillbox. I'll just have to wait until they spot someone else before I make a move."

"Be careful," I yelled, before I realized how stupid that sounded.

"Good lad," Sergeant MacTaggart shouted.

I retrieved my helmet. There was an angry score along one side of it. I put it back on and carefully looked around. Heads were popping up all over and the machine gun was soon occupied with them. Every time it opened up on a target far enough away, Bob would leap up like a demented gopher and hurl himself into the next shell hole. I held my breath every time he moved, but he always made it. In a few more runs he was just 10 feet from the pillbox.

The next time the gun opened up, Bob scuttled forward and tossed two small objects into the black space. A double explosion sounded and I saw a body thrown to one side. Instantly Bob was on the edge of the pillbox firing his rifle down into the nest.

I glanced over at MacTaggart.

"Go on, laddy," he said. "Sounds like yer pal got the job done. Keep the attack going, I'll be fine."

I nodded and scrambled into the open.

Others were doing the same all around. Bob had hauled the German machine gun around and was firing on another machine-gun nest to my left. He was slightly behind it so could fire at the unprotected gunners. The crew soon made a break for the rear, but none of them got very far.

When I reached the pillbox, Bob had stopped firing and was standing there, grinning like an idiot. "It ran out of bullets and I don't know how to load it," he said.

"I think you've done enough. Let's keep going." I slapped Bob on the back. I was ridiculously happy and proud of my friend.

"Jeez," Bob said with a mock stagger. "Don't hit so hard. I don't want to survive the German bullets just to have you break my ribs."

I suppose it was just the wild excitement of still being alive, but I don't ever remember being as happy as I was in that moment. We were actually laughing as we left the ruined pillbox and continued the advance.

That was the pattern for the morning, struggling to keep up with the barrage, being held up by machine guns and continuing once they were cleared. It was slow going, but by 0900 hours we were standing by what was left of Passchendaele church. We had achieved our objectives in only three hours.

We dug in on the far side of the village and waited for counter attacks that never came. It was a rare clear day. A weak sun illuminated a landscape very different from the one we had fought through.

Passchendaele stood on the crest of a low ridge and from it we could look over an almost pastoral view. Nearby, the ground was churned up, but farther away there were almost untouched fields, trees, farm buildings and the distant spires of village churches. I hadn't been in the trenches long, but already I was amazed at the sight of a different world.

"I wonder how MacTaggart is," Bob said as we rested in a shell hole that we had enlarged but not extended far enough to join with manned positions to left and right.

"He'll be fine. The stretcher bearers will have got him back to a field dressing station by now. I don't think it was a really bad wound. Just enough to get him a few weeks in á comfortable hospital bed."

"And some pretty nurses," Bob added.

We both laughed. We still felt stupidly euphoric. We'd just been through a battle in which many, probably hundreds, of our comrades had died or been mutilated, and we were still in far greater danger than we ever would be in civilian life, but we were happy. I felt like a kid at a birthday party. We laughed at the least thing and made silly jokes. One man in our section had found a German helmet with a neat bullet hole right through it. The inside was a mess, but he put it on anyway and made stupid faces and pretended to be the kaiser. We thought it was the funniest thing we had ever seen, better than Charlie Chaplin.

It was partly the release of tension as we realized we had survived, but it was also pride that we Canadians had once more done something special that no one else had. Now the name Passchendaele could be added to that of Vimy Ridge. I felt lucky to be a part of it and wondered how Ken could have been so negative when he talked to me about Vimy.

"They'll probably give you a medal," I said to Bob.

"What for?"

"Taking out that machine-gun nest. It was holding us all up."

"What was I going to do, sit in a muddy shell hole all day listening to you complain? Besides, it wasn't the only nest. Other men must have done just as much in other places. They can't give us all medals."

"We'll see. I reckon you'll get a Military Medal or a Distinguished Conduct Medal. Maybe even a Victoria Cross."

Bob laughed. "I can just see me now, an old man in 1977 in the bar in Moose Jaw, wearing my medal and boring all the young fellas with the same old story of how I took out a German pillbox all those years before." He nudged me in the ribs. "It's a lovely idea, but I plan to be remembered for all the things I do when this war is *over*."

"What do you plan to do?"

"I don't plan to stay in Saskatchewan, that's for sure. Oh, I'll go home and let Mom fuss over me for a while, but I've seen more of the world than I ever imagined, so I can't see me being happy on a quarter section of prairie. Maybe I'll come back and live in Paris, find a beautiful mam'zelle and write a book. I've always enjoyed telling stories and now I'll have something to tell. Funny, eh?" Bob's smile faded and was replaced by a thoughtful expression. "This war's killed millions of boys and young men and caused horrible suffering, yet I can't help feeling that it's the best thing that's ever happened to me."

I was trying to think of a response to this when the whistle of an incoming shell made us both duck. It exploded some distance behind us and was followed by others, but the closest only showered us with clods of dirt. Our artillery was just beginning its response when a figure dove into the trench beside us.

"We have to withdraw right now. There's a massive counter attack coming."

It was Ken. I was horrified to see the state he was in. As usual, he was dressed in a private's uniform so as not to be an obvious target for a German sniper, but his tunic was ragged and torn all down one side and he was without his helmet or rifle. His face beneath his tangled hair was pale and his eyes wide and constantly moving from side to side.

He held his left arm across his chest and his hand jerked spasmodically.

"Ken," I said, forgetting for a moment that I was addressing my commanding officer, "Are you all right? Have you been wounded?"

Ken didn't reply but simply repeated his panicked warning. "The barrage signals an attack coming. We can't hold out here. We have to withdraw. Pass the order along the line!"

"It's all quiet out there, sir," Bob said, peering over the lip of the shell hole. "I don't see any signs of an attack. The German guns have all but stopped firing and ours are giving them quite a pasting, by the sound of it."

"An attack's coming," Ken repeated in a high-pitched whine, ignoring what Bob had said. "We'll all be killed unless we withdraw. I have to tell the others."

He lunged to the side and tried to climb out. Without thinking, I grabbed him and pulled him back in. I was confused, but I knew I couldn't let anyone else see him like this.

"Calm down, Ken. It's all right." My words had no effect and he continued to struggle, kicking me in the shins and trying to wrench himself away. Forgetting that I could be court martialled, even shot, for assaulting an officer, I hauled back and hit

Ken as hard as I could. It was an awkward half-slap, half-punch, and it didn't land cleanly, but it seemed enough to shock him into some kind of awareness. He stopped struggling and looked around as if he had just woken up and wasn't sure where he was. Then he sagged into a heap, as if all his bones had suddenly melted, and began sobbing helplessly.

I looked up at Bob, who was watching, wide-eyed. "Is it still quiet out there?"

Bob peered over the edge of the shell hole and took a quick look around. "It is," he said. "I don't think there's an attack coming."

I crouched down beside Ken and put my arm around his shoulders. "It's all right," I said, as calmly as I could manage. "There's no attack coming. We've taken the village. It's a great victory. Everything'll be fine."

Ken looked up, his filthy face streaked with tears. He was blinking rapidly and his hand was shaking violently. "Fine?" he asked.

"Yes, everything's going to be fine. Even if there is an attack later, we can hold them off. We've won. The Canadians have got the high ground now and no one's going to take it from us."

Ken screwed his eyes tight shut and took a deep breath. He seemed to be searching for strength deep within himself.

"Your uniform's torn," I went on. "Did a shell land near you? Are you wounded?"

He let his breath out and looked at me. "A shell. Yes, that's what happened." He looked down at his shaking left hand as if it belonged to someone else. "Just a few scratches. I'll be all right in a little while."

I sat with Ken in the bottom of our shell hole and talked about our childhood in the Nicola Valley while Bob kept lookout. Whenever a shell exploded nearby, Ken would jump and look around wildly, but he gradually calmed and the shaking lessened.

Eventually he got up. "I have to go and see to the Company," he said. "We need to make sure this line is consolidated and that we're in contact with the units on either side." Talking about military necessities seemed to calm him even more. "Thank you, Allan," he said as he slipped over the edge of the shell hole.

We spent the rest of the afternoon busily digging, and by nightfall we occupied a more or less continuous line. There was a counter attack at dawn the next day, but with the help of our artillery, we easily repulsed it. On November 10 some of the 1st Division attacked to the north of us, but made no progress. Four days later we were relieved and sent back down to the Front near Vimy to wait out the winter.

I saw little of Ken those days and wondered if he was avoiding me, embarrassed by his breakdown. The times I did see him, he appeared to be functioning normally and it was only because I knew him so well that I could spot the lack of his old humorous optimism, and that occasional twitch of the left hand that he cleverly turned into a gesture. I worried about him, but there seemed little I could do, so I just got on with life.

Chapter 7
Waiting
Near Vimy, Winter 1917–18

We spent the winter digging, carrying, waiting and being bored. The only entertainment was burning lice out of the seams of our clothes over a candle flame, and hunting rats the size of cats. Our casualties were replaced by kids recently out from home and training with the 5th Division in England. We watched them settle into the endless repetition of a few days in the front line, a few in reserve and a few in rest. Bob and I and the others marvelled at how naïve the newcomers were and how stupid they seemed, not knowing things that were second nature to us old hands.

Sergeant MacTaggart rejoined us from his stay in hospital in mid-December, with stories about the church bells being rung in England after the tanks had broken through the German lines at Cambrai in November. He said a lot of people had thought the war was as good as over, but the Germans counter attacked and all the gains of the first few days had to be given up. We laughed when we heard how optimistic people in England were. We were still waiting for that black flare at midnight.

About the time MacTaggart returned, it was announced that Bob had been awarded the Distinguished Conduct Medal for taking out the machine-gun nest outside Passchendaele. I was excited; the DCM was almost as high an honour as the Victoria Cross, but Bob passed it off lightly.

"They gave me a medal," he said, grinning, when the rest of the platoon congratulated him, "simply because you lot were too lazy to do your jobs properly. Personally, I'd rather have an increase in pay, a clean uniform without any lice in it and two weeks in Paris."

After Passchendaele, Ken was away on a lot of courses — communications, tactics and so on — so I didn't see much of him. When I did, I watched him closely, searching for signs of a repeat of the breakdown in the shell hole. I made no attempt to talk to him. We had grown apart.

I had spent most of my life trying to imitate Ken. He was the reason I was in the war at all. To see him weeping and shaking uncontrollably in the shell hole had been horrifying. I felt betrayed that he had turned out to be a coward. He was nothing like the brave soldiers I had read about in all my adventure books — he didn't deserve to be an officer in the Canadian army.

I suppose I knew, deep down, that it wasn't that simple, that soldiers weren't either brave and cheerful like Bob or snivelling cowards like Ken, but back then I wasn't prepared to make any allowances. I wanted life to be simple.

In my letters home, life *was* simple. I always worked hard at making the letters cheerful and full of amusing little stories about what the men in my platoon were getting up to.

I remember writing a long letter about our Christmas dinner when we were at rest behind the lines and our meal was a large goose that Neil Page, a lad from Vancouver with a knack for "finding" useful things, had somehow acquired from a French farmhouse. On Christmas Eve, Neil had shown up at our billet with the goose in a huge sack slung over his shoulder.

"Look what I've got, boys," he said proudly as he opened the neck of the sack and upended it.

The goose fell out and, almost the instant it hit the ground, exploded with an ear-splitting series of honks and took off across country. Led by Bob, about twenty men did a very passable impression of the Keystone Cops as they collided with each other in their haste to catch it while Neil stood stupidly repeating, "But I wrung its neck."

The goose was eventually recaptured and its neck properly wrung. It made a wonderful meal and we had the added bonus of being able to tease Neil for his incompetence.

I wrote home about this scene at great length, but never mentioned that, the week after New Year's, Neil had had his brains smeared over the trench wall by a sniper. I was doing in my letters home exactly what Ken had done in his letters to me. It is simply not possible to describe Hell to those who have not been there.

Oddly, I didn't derive much pleasure from the letters I received from home. It was good to hear that Mom and Dad were fine and that the farm was doing well, but their talk of how the weather was affecting the crops or of Dad's trip to Kamloops to look at buying a new tractor was from a different world. It all seemed so pointless and unimportant. I knew it would never be possible to make people understand my world, either its horrors or its black humour, but I was beginning to wonder if it would ever again be possible for me to understand the world that normal people lived in.

On top of that, my nightmares got worse as winter progressed. Mostly they were made up of visions from my experiences in war — the bloody Red Cap's face at Etaples, the rotting German body from the trench wall, or Lofty with half his head blown away.

New scenes — a man with his face torn off by a piece of shrapnel and another who had his leg blown off and who, completely conscious and rational, bled slowly to death on the floor of our trench as we watched helplessly — added themselves to my nighttime imaginings.

At first I discounted my dreams as simple stress, but as the cold, rainy winter dragged on they became more vivid and frequent. Oddly, they were worse when we were at rest and safe, probably because I had more time to dwell on things. I found myself fearful of going to sleep, but that didn't help, since the less I slept the more I dreamed when exhaustion finally did overcome me.

I told no one about my dreams, not even Bob, but as spring approached and they became more frequent, I noticed that I would occasionally twitch for no reason or jump at the least sound. I was also becoming short-tempered.

Bob and another prairie boy called Chris were the comedians of our platoon, always fooling around and springing practical jokes on people. Once they found Sergeant MacTaggart asleep in a barn. They propped empty wine bottles all round him and made him look as if he had fallen asleep drunk.

Another time they developed a list of "soldiers' superstitions," some of which were:

1. It is unlucky for 13 men to sit down for a meal when rations have only been issued for 7.
2. It is bad luck (for your mate) if you drop your rifle on his foot.
3. It is bad luck (for you) if you drop your rifle on the sergeant's foot.
4. It is bad luck to be called to hear a lecture on the glorious history of the Regiment. It means that there is a battle coming.
5. It is unlucky to visit the latrines during a barrage.
6. It is unlucky to take a stroll in daylight in no man's land when enemy snipers are awake.

The list became very popular with the Company and it seemed every soldier had his favourite to add.

One cold and rainy day, after I had woken up from an especially bad dream and was feeling unusually miserable, Bob and Chris came up to me as I was struggling to heat up some water for tea.

"Ah, tea," Bob said. "I'll have a mug of that."

I wanted nothing more than to be left alone, so I simply grunted.

"*He's* happy this morning," Chris added. "The funk-hole in the Savoy Hotel not to your liking?"

I really wasn't in the mood for mindless banter, so I ignored them both, but they sat down beside me on the fire-step and kept talking.

"I heard a new superstition from the fellows who brought up the rolls of barbed wire last night," Bob said. "Best yet, I reckon. Apparently, it's very bad luck to be killed on a Friday."

Bob chuckled away to himself, but I had had enough. None of this war had turned out as I had expected. The rats, the lice, the filth, the bad food — when there was food at all— the utter boredom of the same routine day after day and, on top of it all, Ken was a coward. Everything seemed much more complicated and frightening than I felt I could handle and I couldn't even escape into sleep. I suddenly felt completely overwhelmed by things I couldn't control.

I turned on Bob and Chris. "Go to hell! Both of you," I hissed, loudly enough for a couple of soldiers along the trench to look up in surprise. "I'm sick of your stupid superstitions and stupid attitude. Why can't you just leave me alone?"

Bob winced as if I had hit him. Chris took a step back and put his hands up in supplication. "All right, mate," he said. "I'm gone," and he turned and stalked off down the trench.

Bob stayed and stared at me. He had the sense not to try and talk to me in the mood I was in, and I had almost calmed enough to apologize when he too turned on his heel and left me to my misery and my lukewarm tea.

Chris usually avoided me after that, but I apologized later to Bob. He said it was okay, just as he had done the other times I had blown up for no apparent reason. He even tried to talk to me about it, but I brushed him off.

I wanted to talk to Ken. He was the only person I had ever spoken to about my feelings, but he was a coward, so I just continued in my loneliness, hoping things would get better. Then, in early March, everything changed.

Over the previous few weeks, there had been a lot of talk about the Germans launching a big offensive to try to end the war before the American army got too strong. Certainly they had a lot of extra troops now that Russia wasn't fighting any more, and they would use those troops somewhere. The pessimists who had talked about the war going on forever now began to talk about the war ending this year — with the *Germans* victorious. Most of us didn't believe that, but there was an uncertainty in the air.

In March Ken returned from a briefing at headquarters and announced that our Company was to move south of Arras, away from the rest of the Canadian Corps, to spend a few days on the British 3rd Army Front to learn the new techniques that were being used for defence. The idea was that, over the spring, selected units would see the new methods for themselves and then return to teach them to the rest. However, before we left we had one last task to perform.

Ken looked very nervous as he announced that he had been ordered to lead a raid across no man's land that night. Apparently there was a lot of activity going on behind the German lines opposite us — troop and gun movements — and we had to capture a soldier for interrogation to see if this had anything to do with the coming attack.

Around midnight the section congregated in the trench. Our faces were blackened and we carried the minimum of equipment. Many men even left their rifles behind, preferring a selection of clubs and knives, which would be much more use if we got into a fight in the close confines of the enemy trenches. Even before we climbed out of our trench, I could see that Ken was in trouble. His hands were shaking violently and he had a nervous tic beneath his left eye. Sergeant Mac-Taggart spotted it too, and calmly took charge.

"With yer permission, sir?" he asked Ken. Ken nodded. "We'll make this quick and easy. Over there, grab some lonely sentry in a sap dreaming of being home in Berlin, and get back over here. No heroics." He glanced at Bob, who smiled. "Just keep low and follow the captain and me. If you hear a flare going up, drop. And freeze. It's movement the sentry'll see." He saluted Ken and added, "The men're ready, sir."

It looked as if it was a great effort for Ken to speak, but he managed a halting, "Very good, Sergeant. Thank you. Follow me."

We climbed the ladders and threaded our way along the marked paths through our wire. It was a rare, clear night, but the moon was new and the darkness almost total. We had to concentrate to keep close to the slightly darker shapes of our companions. We moved so slowly it took almost an hour to cross the 250 yards of no man's land.

Eventually, responding to touch signals we

had learned ahead of time, we all stopped and lay still, listening. I could hear Ken breathing hard and rapidly beside me and hoped it didn't sound as loud to a German sentry. Other sounds came from farther away, the metallic rattle of a mess tin against a rifle barrel, a cough, a curse in German. I knew the plan was for MacTaggart, Bob and a few other men to drop into a German sap, knock out the sentry and then haul him back to our lines. The rest of us were there to help if things went wrong, so all we could do at this point was wait and keep quiet.

I lost all sense of time. My shoulders began to ache with the tension and my eyes stung as I strained to see through the darkness. I felt Ken move beside me and heard a whisper in my ear. "I think we're discovered," he said. "We should pull back."

Ken was speaking very quietly. I could feel his breath on my ear, but it almost sounded like he was screaming.

"Shhh," I whispered back. "We have to wait till they bring back the prisoner."

"They should have one by now," Ken said. Even in a whisper, I could hear the quaver in his voice. "Something's gone wrong."

I didn't want to get into an argument with Ken and was worried that he might do something stupid. I was debating what to do when I heard a brief scuffle to my right. There was a distinct *thump* followed by a soft grunt.

"What's that?" Ken asked nervously.

"I think that's our prisoner," I replied. A moment later I saw a group of darker shapes coming towards us. A low whistle told me it was Bob and the others returning. They were dragging something. When they reached us we rose and headed back to our trenches.

We were less concerned about being discovered on the way back and moved much faster. The main danger was that the missing sentry would be noticed. I judged that we were about halfway back when I heard a shout followed by the low hiss of a flare. I flopped down and an instant later a brilliant white light, like a photographer's flash, turned everything into harsh daylight or impenetrable shadow.

My head was turned to the left and I could see the lumps of other bodies around me. Mac-Taggart, Bob and two other men were holding down a figure in a field-grey uniform. Ken was some way back, more in a crouch than lying flat. Then I saw Chris. He was standing beside Ken, almost upright in mid-step, like a perfectly carved statue. "Don't move," I heard MacTaggart say. There was no need for silence now. "When the flare dies, head for our trench. The boys there'll give us covering fire."

The flare was already fading when a machine gun began to clatter. It was probably just spraying randomly, but several bullets caught Chris across the chest. He slumped to the ground and I heard Ken say, "My God."

Darkness, utterly black after the flare, descended as MacTaggart shouted orders. "Whoever's closest, grab that wounded man. Let's move before the next flare goes up."

I rose and began moving but I hadn't taken more than five or six steps before I heard the telltale hiss. I flopped down.

The scene in the harsh glare of the flare was similar to before, except that everyone had moved forward. Everyone except Ken. He was frozen in the same crouching position, in the same place as before, Chris's body beside him.

Our raid had woken a hornet's next of activity and the firing was much heavier than before. Rifles cracked and machine guns rattled on both sides all along the Front and were joined by the occasional *crump* of exploding mortar shells.

I was debating whether to go back and get Ken when I saw him slowly stand up and look around as if waking from a dream.

"Get down!" I yelled.

Ken looked over at me and began a slow walk forward. He had covered about half the distance to my position when a bullet caught him, spinning him round so that he fell on his back. Without thinking, I bolted up, ran the few steps to Ken and threw myself down beside him.

"I've done enough," Ken said in a faraway voice. "It's time to go home."

"Yes it is," I agreed, not knowing what else to say. "I'll get you home."

As the flare faded, I shoved my hands under Ken's armpits and began hauling. It was slow going and I had to flop down every time another flare went up, but eventually we made it through the wire and tumbled into our own trench.

Ken screamed in pain as he landed on his face on the duckboards of the trench floor, but before I could respond, MacTaggart was beside us. "Get a stretcher," he shouted, as he cut open Ken's blood-stained uniform.

There was a neat, round hole in Ken's back, on the right side. Ragged pieces of his uniform had been pushed into the hole, but there was surprisingly little blood. MacTaggart placed a field dressing on it.

"Hold that in place while we turn him over," he ordered me. "And keep it tight on there."

I pressed the dressing to the wound and shifted my own position as MacTaggart rolled Ken over. There was a much larger, more irregular hole in Ken's front and it was bleeding freely. Within the mess of ragged flesh and pieces of material, I could see jagged fragments of white bone sticking out. MacTaggart wrapped bandages around Ken's body to hold the dressings in place, but in moments they were soaked in blood.

"Where's that bloody stretcher?" MacTaggart shouted.

Ken was conscious and looking round. "I'm going home," he said.

"That's right, sir," MacTaggart answered.

"It's a long walk," Ken said. His speech was becoming slurred.

"You won't have to walk," MacTaggart said. "There's a stretcher coming."

As if in response, two men appeared round the fire bay carrying a rolled stretcher. With some effort they unrolled it and we managed to get Ken onto it. As the bearers lifted him, Ken looked at me, smiled and said, "I stood up." Then he was gone, the bearers awkwardly lifting him above their heads to turn corners in the trench.

The next while was busy. Chris had been brought in farther down the trench, but he was already dead.

Bob was assigned to escort the German prisoner back to headquarters.

I sat on the fire-step, trying to collect my thoughts. I was worried sick about Ken. He might be a coward, but he was still my friend and the wound had looked bad. The chances of infection were high anyway, and who knew what internal damage the bullet had done.

Then the last thing Ken had said surfaced in my memory. What had he meant by telling me he had stood up? I replayed the scene in no man's land in my head. Ken hadn't moved between the first two flares. He had held his frozen position, but then when he was *exposed*, he had stood up.

A chill ran up my back as I realized what Ken had done. He had tried to kill himself. He had intended for the Germans to kill him. But why? Had he reached a place of so much terror that he couldn't stand it anymore? I didn't know, but the more I replayed the scene, the more certain I became that his action was deliberate. That's what he had been telling me as he was carried away. Silently, I prayed that he had failed.

The next morning I received a letter from home telling me what a good harvest it had been that fall and that Becky Bly, a war widow from up the Valley, had married Robert Pritchard, a local businessman, in the biggest wedding the area had seen in years. I got halfway through my mother's description of Becky's wedding dress before I crumpled the letter and shoved it into the mud.

Chapter 8
Hell
Near Arras, March 21, 1918

In the dream I was lying on the hill where I shot the deer. I knew that I had already hit it and should go down and finish it off, but I was paralyzed. The deer, bleeding profusely from my bullet wound in its side and dragging its useless back legs, was coming up the hill towards me, and it wasn't alone.

Away from the deer on either side stretched a line composed of every dead soldier I had seen. Most were horribly mutilated, but they kept coming anyway. Even the man whose legs had been blown off by a shell dragged himself towards me at the same relentless pace as the others.

I didn't know why they were all coming for me, but I knew that it wasn't a good reason and that, if I was to have any chance of surviving the war, I had to stop them. I aimed my rifle and fired at each horror in turn, but they kept coming. My bullets hit the mark every time and tore off pieces of flesh and bone, but nothing slowed them down.

With each shot they came closer and I became more panicked. I felt sweat breaking out all over my body and my breathing became fast and shallow. I had to stop them. I fired steadily and accurately. Oddly, I never had to reload. But nothing worked. The tattered bodies of the dead approached relentlessly.

The deer in the centre of the line was barely five feet away from me when I woke up gasping for breath. I threw myself out of my funk-hole in a panic and stood in the trench, struggling to calm down. It was still dark but work was going on all around me. Men were moving back and forth, carrying wire and shovels to wherever they were needed. I wasn't involved because I had been on guard duty earlier and had been allowed a short rest. I wished now that I had volunteered to repair the trench rather than sleep.

I stood on the fire-step to get out of the way and peered to the east. It was still dark, but I could see the swirls of a thick fog all around. Everything was quiet. I shivered as the sweat cooled on my body. My breathing had calmed and the fear I had woken with dissipated, but the feeling of utter helplessness from the dream lingered. I had to stop that line of dead coming for me and I tried hard to fight them off, but nothing worked. With every dream, the corpses got closer before I woke up. What would happen when they reached me? Would that be a sign that I was going to die?

The rumours of a coming German attack were stronger now, but no one knew exactly where, and there were no signs that it was imminent here.

We had arrived the day before, March 20, and taken over a stretch of trench in the so-called Battle Zone. The idea now was no longer to pack the front-line trenches with soldiers and try and hold them to the last man. Barrages had become so heavy that the front-line trenches, and all the men in them, could be wiped out even before an attack started. The new word was "elasticity." When an attack was expected, only a few soldiers would man the front-line trench, but they would be supported by a number of defensive zones — the Forward Zone, immediately behind the front-line trench; the Battle Zone, a mile or so back; and the Support Zone, another mile behind that.

Each zone had all the usual barbed wire and deep trenches, but behind that were defensive positions designed to hold out even if cut off and attacked from all sides. The idea was that the Forward Zone would be fairly lightly defended and the enemy would be drawn on into the Battle Zone, where they would be stopped.

"Couldn't sleep, eh?"

I turned to see Bob standing beside me. Good, steadfast, reliable Bob. However much I swore at him and told him to leave me alone, he was always there for me with a pat on the back or a joke. Sometimes it annoyed me, but mostly it helped my mood and I was glad that someone cared, even if I couldn't bring myself to tell him what was troubling me.

"No. Too much going on," I said. "You reckon they'll attack while we're here?"

"No sign of it," Bob replied, gazing out into the fog. "We'll only be here for a couple of days and their artillery hasn't been firing any ranging shots on our guns or trenches, so they can't be planning a barrage any time soon."

"But they will attack eventually?" I asked.

"Sure. Every day there are more Yanks here and the German prisoners the trench raids bring in are younger and less well fed. They say the blockade of the German ports is really starting to hurt and that the civilians are near starvation. If Gerry doesn't win the war soon, they never will.

"I know people say the war will go on into 1919 at least, but I reckon if we can hold off the attack this spring, they might collapse."

"I hope so."

"Then we can all go home as heroes." Bob laughed and clapped me on the back.

"You can," I said. "You've got a medal and plans to see the world and do something with your life. What can I do?"

"Anything you want. There won't be any officers to tell you what to do."

"I know that, but I left the Nicola Valley to see the world. Mostly all I've seen are ruins and the insides of trenches. When I joined up I thought being in the war would be a big adventure, the beginning of a new, exciting life. But it's not. It's just boredom, misery and death."

"Wow, Allan, what's eating you?"

I decided then that I would tell Bob about my dreams. The weight of them was becoming too much to bear and, even if I could bring myself to talk to Ken, for all I knew, he was dead.

"I'm having these dreams . . . " I said.

I could feel Bob looking at me, but I kept staring to the front.

"I assume these aren't about that pretty nurse at the hospital where we were in reserve last week?"

"No. These are about the dead. Every dead man I've ever seen is in them and they are coming for me. Getting closer every dream. I'm scared of what will happen when they reach me."

"Jesus," Bob said softly. "How long have you been having these dreams?"

I explained about going deer hunting with Ken.

"And you're worried that when they reach you, that will be a sign that you're going to die?" Bob asked.

"Yes, but I'm more scared that they mean I'm going to go mad or end up a coward like Ken. I'm terrified of breaking down like he did."

Bob was silent for a moment. "You know," he said eventually, "you called me a hero, but it didn't take any courage to do what I did. If anything, I was stupid. I didn't think, I just acted. I would have been much braver if I had realized the dangers and still gone ahead. Remember, Ken has been out here much longer than us. He held it together for three years. Even after his breakdown in that shell hole at Passchendaele, he managed to function for months, organizing and taking responsibility for the whole Company. Perhaps it takes more courage to do that, to just keep going when you know you're falling apart, than it does to do one spectacular thing."

"Okay," I agreed, "but he broke down completely in the end. He was deliberately trying to kill himself when he stood up on that raid."

"Maybe bravery isn't enough. Maybe every-body has a limit, and when you reach that, no matter how brave you might be, your mind and your body simply say 'Enough.' They take over and do whatever they can to get you out of that situation."

I was thinking about what Bob had said when Sergeant MacTaggart came up.

"Come on, lads. There's plenty work to be done before it gets light."

I had turned to get off the fire-step when Bob said, "What do you suppose *that* means?"

I twisted back in the direction he was looking, to see a single white flare arcing into the dark sky above the fog.

"A signal," MacTaggart said. "Not a good sign."

The flash came first. As far as we could see in either direction, the horizon lit up brightly enough to show through the fog. Then came the sound.

In every other artillery barrage I had been through, it had been possible to distinguish indi-vidual guns, the deep snarl of the heavy howitzers and the higher-pitched howl of the smaller field guns and mortars. This morning there was just one sudden, overwhelming roar, as if the very earth were tearing itself apart.

We should have ducked down, but the awesome

magnitude of what we were seeing and hearing froze us in place. I barely had time for the odd thought that this sounded like a huge avalanche coming towards us when the British Forward Zone exploded. It was about two thousand yards away from us and we could see no details through the fog, but the simultaneous arrival of hundreds of tons of high explosives, shrapnel and gas shells was breathtaking.

Even at that distance, the ground shook so hard that we instinctively grabbed onto the trench wall. The flashes of the high explosives through the fog looked like a lightning storm over the horizon and vast gouts of flame and columns of earth rose into the sky everywhere. The fog took on a greenish tinge from the poison gas.

"Those poor sods," MacTaggart said.

It took me a moment to realize that he was talking about the British soldiers cowering beneath the storm we were witnessing.

"Why aren't they shelling us?" Bob asked.

"They will, lad," MacTaggart said. "Ye can be sure of that. As soon as they're done with those boys, it'll be our turn."

The thought that we would have to go through the hell we were witnessing sent a shudder of fear right through me. My stomach felt as though it had turned to water and my legs twitched as if they wanted to start running.

"What can we do?" I asked.

"When the time comes, get yer head down and pray."

"MacTaggart!"

I looked over to see the lieutenant coming down the trench. "Get the men into the bottom of the trench with their gas helmets ready, and set sentries to watch for an attack."

"Aye, sir." MacTaggart saluted and addressed us. "You heard the officer. Get down there and if I find any of you without yer gas helmet, you'll wish the Gerries had found you first."

We sat on the fire-step, hugging our gas helmets and rifles, and waited as the ground shook below us and the sky roared above. Countless German shells formed a canopy over us as they roared towards our guns, communications and headquarters.

The waiting was the worst. I sat for what I thought was an hour, only to look at my watch and see that less than five minutes had passed. Perhaps I didn't have to wait for the dead of my dreams to reach me. Perhaps the dream I had just had was the signal that I was about to die. My imagination began to get out of hand. I saw ugly black pieces of metal fly through the air towards me and felt them tear off my arms and legs and punch great gaping holes in my chest and stomach. I was overcome with an almost uncontrollable desire to run, anywhere to get away from here.

"After this is all over — " I felt Bob's comforting hand on my shoulder " — the war, I mean. Why don't we stick together and see a bit of the world that's not the back wall of a muddy trench?"

I looked round at Bob. Was he serious? Was he really talking about a time after this?

"Of course, I'd insist that we go to Paris first," he said with a smile. "That's my dream and I claim priority, but I'll let you have second choice. Where shall we go after we tire of the mam'zelles of the Moulin Rouge?"

I stared at him. It took me a long time to work out what he was saying, but he waited and nodded encouragement.

"Spain," I said eventually. "I read a book once about the Moors and Granada. The palace there is one of the wonders of the world."

"Spain it is then, Allan. Then it'll be my turn again. I think we should head over to Egypt after that. I've always had a yearning to see the pyramids." Bob poked me in the ribs with his elbow. "I wonder if the Egyptian women are all as beautiful as that Nefertiti?"

"Probably not," I said, so seriously that Bob burst out laughing. It was an effort to concentrate, but his conversation was giving me something other than the shelling and my dreams to focus on.

I was trying to think of somewhere we could go after Egypt when I realized that the barrage had stopped. Hundreds of shells were still flying overhead and bursting to our rear, but the pounding of the Forward Zone had ceased.

"Are they going to attack?" I asked, panic flooding through me.

"Quiet," MacTaggart ordered.

At first I couldn't hear anything other than the distant explosions, but I gradually began to make out a soft popping noise closer by. I was about to ask if anyone else could hear it when MacTaggart stood up.

"Gas, lads," he shouted. "Put on yer helmets. Now!"

We fumbled for our cumbersome respirators as MacTaggart stood beating out a warning on the empty shell casing that was hung outside the dugout entrance. Behind him I could see a thicker wall of fog rolling towards us down the trench. A figure was just visible inside the cloud, staggering from side to side and clutching his throat.

The mournful *clang* of MacTaggart's gas alarm echoed while I struggled into my helmet. My eyes were watering and the sharp metallic taste of the gas was catching at the back of my throat by the time I had the helmet in place. Suddenly I was cut off from the world around me. I could still hear the explosions, but they were muffled and my vision was limited to a cloudy area directly ahead of me. I felt trapped and had a strong urge to vomit.

Bob tapped my shoulder and gave me a thumbs-up. As I returned the gesture I noticed that my hand was shaking.

There was no bright flash to announce the new barrage, simply an ear-splitting roar that enveloped us all instantly. It was like being in the eye of a hurricane; all around us was chaos and destruction. I couldn't even think.

Shells were landing all along the barbed-wire entanglements in front of the trench, throwing up great fountains of earth, shattered wooden stakes and chaotic tangles of wire. Other, heavier guns were targeting the fortified strongpoints behind us. It was as if God were angry with the earth itself and had determined that nothing was to be allowed to live on it. And yet, deep in our trench, we were safe from all but a direct hit.

Instinctively we huddled down as low as possible in the bottom of the trench as the ground heaved and clods of earth fell off the trench walls and flew through the air.

How long that second barrage lasted I have no idea. It seemed like weeks. The sound was a physical presence — a hammer beating constantly inside my head. I was an animal, nothing more, numb and helpless, watching my left hand shake and wondering vaguely who it belonged to. After a while a nursery rhyme from my childhood, "Baa Baa Black Sheep," began to run endlessly round my head. I think I screamed it out loud into my mask.

The need to vomit was almost irresistible. I must have inhaled more gas than I thought. I was suffocating. I wanted more than anything to rip my gas helmet off. A tiny rational part of my brain knew that I had to keep the helmet on, but my terror was close to making me rip it off. I was breathing dangerously fast, yet everything seemed to be happening in slow motion.

I looked around wildly. The masked figures crowded on the floor of the trench didn't even look human. We were a herd of animals with squat snouts and wide, staring glass eyes, huddled in a poisonous, swirling fog, waiting for some vast predator to come and feed on us.

Only MacTaggart, recognizable by the sergeant's stripes on his sleeve, was on his feet, moving back and forth along the trench, checking that gas helmets were secure and encouraging the men. He bent down, patted Bob on the shoulder and gave me a thumbs-up.

As he straightened up, a shell exploded on the parapet. Whether it was the force of the blast or a piece of shrapnel, I have no idea, but MacTaggart's head disappeared. There was a red haze. Then, suddenly, there was only the torn remnants of his neck, and blood pouring down his uniform. The body stood for an incredibly long time, as if trying to decide what to do, then slowly sat down on the trench floor with its back resting against the parados.

I felt no shock, but simply watched what happened with detached interest. I was vaguely sorry that MacTaggart was dead, I had liked him.

I felt Bob move beside me. He entered my restricted field of vision and knelt beside Mac-Taggart's body. That's stupid, I thought sluggishly, you can't live without a head and even a hero can't put one back on once it's been blown off.

Bob stood up and turned to me. Very slowly, he removed his gas helmet. I wanted to say stop, or prevent him from doing it, but my mouth couldn't form words and my body felt as if it were made of lead.

Bob looked at me. I could see his mouth moving, but I was deaf. He stepped over to me. For a terrifying moment I thought the gas had killed him and he was one of the corpses in my dream come to get me, but he bent down, shook my shoulders and shouted in my ear. He must have shouted but his voice sounded thin and very far away. "It's all right," he said. "The gas has gone."

Gradually the meaning of the words dawned on me and I fumbled to get my mask off. I felt free. The smell and taste of the gas were still in the air, but the clouds I had seen advancing down the trench had dispersed. Even the fog had thinned. To my surprise, it was full daylight. We must have been huddled in the trench for hours. I grinned, stupidly. Mindless joy swept over me. I had survived.

"I think it means they're going to attack." Bob stood on the fire-step and peered carefully over the edge while I struggled to understand what he had said. Eventually I joined him.

The barrage had moved back to the Forward Zone, or perhaps it had been there all along while we hid.

"As long as they keep shelling the front lines,"

Bob said, thinking out loud, "they won't attack. They would never send their men into that."

As if the Germans had been listening, the shelling in front of us stopped and explosions began again around us. In an instant my joy evaporated as if it had never existed. It wasn't fair. I had survived the barrage. The Germans weren't allowed to shell me again. I felt tears sliding down my cheeks. I had to leave. I couldn't go through this again.

Calmly I stepped onto the floor of the trench, carefully placed my rifle against the parapet and began walking away. I heard Bob shouting for me to stop, but I ignored him. The desire to leave, to be anywhere but here, was irresistible.

I felt Bob grab my shoulders. "Where are you going?" he yelled. I shook him off and kept on. He pushed past me and stood in my way. "You can't go! It's desertion!"

Anger blinded me. What right did Bob have to stop me? Just because he had done something foolish and been given a medal for it didn't give him the right to prevent me doing what I wanted, and I wanted above anything else in the world to get away from here.

I swung my fist as hard as I could. I doubt if it was a very well-coordinated blow, but it took Bob completely by surprise. My fist connected with his jaw and he fell backwards with a startled look on his face. Then the sandbags of the parapet to my right bulged out towards me. Something hit me on the side of my head and everything went black.

Chapter 9
Escape
Near Arras, March 21, 1918

The dream came again, but this time the horrors reached me. I wanted to run, but I couldn't. A great weight was pressing on my legs. I lay in helpless panic as the deer gnawed at my cheek with its blunt teeth. Around me, men leered with half-blown-away features and pawed at me with shattered hands. I screamed but my mouth filled with dirt. I could move my arms and fought to push the deer away from me.

I came to, scrabbling at the dirt that covered my face. I turned my head and vomited out the earth that filled my mouth and gasped in a lungful of air. I opened my eyes and saw a startlingly blue strip of sky, streaked with grey tendrils of smoke. I gradually became aware of something close to silence. Shells exploded in the distance and a machine gun clacked somewhere, but the intense barrage had stopped. As my mind reasserted itself, my fear returned. I remembered that I had to escape.

My legs were buried but I sat up in a cascade of dirt and looked around. The first thing I saw was MacTaggart's headless body sitting across from me. I twisted to my left, ignoring the sharp pain that seared through my head. A large section of the parapet had collapsed in a confusion of earth, stones and ripped sandbags almost filling the bottom of the trench. I twisted the opposite way and saw even worse destruction. The trench was half filled with rubble and that was what was trapping my legs. Near where I assumed my knees must be, a hand and forearm extended up from the collapse, the fingers curled in supplication.

"Bob!" I screamed. Memory flooded back. I had hit him and he had fallen onto the floor of the trench at the instant a shell had collapsed the parapet. It must be him buried there.

I reached over as far as I could and grasped the hand. It returned my grip. I pulled as hard as I could, but it was solidly embedded. Like a madman, I dug through the dirt around the arm. I reached the elbow, but I couldn't stretch farther.

I wildly began digging at my legs, throwing dirt and stones everywhere. Pieces of buried metal cut me, fragments of barbed wire stabbed me and my fingernails broke and tore, but I kept on. Eventually, I reached my knees and kicked the rest of the dirt away. Rolling over, I grabbed Bob's hand. This time there was no response. I dug like a crazed dog. I uncovered the rest of Bob's arm, his shoulder and, finally, his face.

Bob looked as if he were asleep, except for a blueish tinge to his skin. I cleaned as much dirt as I could out of his nose and mouth and shook him gently.

"Come on, Bob," I said. "Wake up. I'm sorry I hit you."

I was mad then, sitting in a ruined trench in the midst of a battle, talking to Bob as if he were about to make a joke of the whole thing. I suppose insanity was better than acknowledging that I had killed him. If I hadn't punched him, he wouldn't have been on the floor of the trench when the parapet collapsed. He would have survived.

Tears streamed down my face, but whether from crying or the effects of the lingering gas, I had no idea. I was vaguely aware of things going on around me, men rolling out of funk-holes or emerging from dugouts, orders being shouted and scattered rifle and machine-gun fire from all along the line, but it was all happening very far away, to someone else. The only thing that was important to me was sitting and talking to Bob.

"The attack's coming now. Get onto the fire-step." The voice sounded distant but I could feel breath and spit on my ear. I looked round to see the lieutenant crouching over me. I knew him well, but I couldn't remember his name. "Can you hear me?" he yelled.

I nodded slowly.

"Then find a rifle and get up on the fire-step."

"I can't," I said, forming every word painfully slowly. "I have to talk to Bob."

The lieutenant glanced at Bob's dead face and slapped my cheek hard. The pain brought me back somewhere close to reality.

"Get a rifle and get onto the fire-step." The lieutenant moved off barking orders at other stunned men.

Sluggishly I obeyed, picked up MacTaggart's discarded rifle and peered out over no man's land.

Streams of black smoke drifted across my view and a pall of dust hung above the Forward Zone. Occasional shrapnel shells — whether ours or the Germans', I had no idea — exploded in the air in peaceful-looking puffs of white. Heavy explosions echoed from far behind us. Our wire was almost completely destroyed and huge craters were everywhere, but grass still grew between them.

"Look!" someone yelled.

I tensed and peered hard.

"It's a hare."

There it was, a large hare, unhurt but disoriented and with eyes wide with fear, hopping back and forth through the torn wire.

"Look, Bob," I said under my breath, "a hare. I wonder how it survived." Then, "Good luck," I said more loudly.

"Here they come!" the lieutenant yelled.

The Germans didn't come at us in the waves that the old soldiers talked about from the early years of the war, but in small groups, darting from shell hole to shell hole. Rifle fire opened up all along the line and I heard the harsh clatter of a Lewis gun.

Everything seemed to be happening in slow motion and none of it involved me. It was like being in a dream, except it was not nearly as frightening as the dreams I had been having.

"Well, this is a real battle, Bob," I said.

I saw one German soldier in a crouching run. His rifle was slung over his back and he held one of the long-handled German grenades in each hand. Others were stuffed into the tops of his boots. I fired and he disappeared from sight, but I don't think I hit him. My left hand was shaking too much for a steady aim.

The first grenade exploded in the trench to my right. I felt its blast pull at my trouser legs and a clod of earth pounded me on the shoulder. Someone screamed. I glanced round to see a crumpled body on the trench floor and the lieutenant sitting on the fire-step, his uniform jacket in tatters and blood pouring down his face.

"Brown," I said. "That's the lieutenant's name, Bob. Lieutenant Brown. I'd forgotten. Why didn't you tell me? I think he's from Orillia."

"They're in the trench!" someone yelled.

A German soldier appeared around the corner of our fire bay, pulling a grenade from his boot. He was a small man and his coal-scuttle helmet looked ridiculously large on his head. He was wearing thick spectacles with round lenses.

I turned towards him, aimed my rifle and fired. Nothing happened. I'd forgotten to work the bolt and eject the old cartridge after I'd shot at the man attacking across no man's land.

The German soldier stared at me, the grenade held above his head. His eyes were huge through his spectacles. He must have been in shock, thinking he was about to die. Before he could recover or I could work the rifle bolt, the lieutenant rose from the fire-step and forced his bayonet up hard into the man's stomach and under his ribs.

A look of surprise crossed the soldier's face and he coughed, almost politely. A trickle of blood ran down his chin and he sagged to the floor of the trench like a sack of discarded rags. The grenade fell out of his hand, bounced in the dirt and came to rest beside Bob's head.

The lieutenant looked at me and smiled. The grenade exploded.

The blast hurled me backwards and forced the breath out of my chest. I lay, gasping like a stranded fish, struggling to suck air into my lungs. My helmet had been blown off and something had hit me on the temple. My head hurt unbearably and something warm was trickling down the side of my face.

The lieutenant's body lay on the trench floor, the dead German across his legs, but I ignored everything. The only thing I had to do was see if Bob was all right. I stood up. Pain pounded through my head and I had to close my eyes and lean against the trench wall. Carefully I opened my eyes and worked my way over to where Bob's face still stared out of the collapsed parapet.

"I'll go and get help," I said. "There's Germans all around, so lie still and keep quiet. I'll be back as soon as I can."

I patted Bob's cheek. It felt oddly cold and

clammy. "Try and keep warm," I said, and then I just walked away.

I was fixated on the idea of getting help for Bob, but somehow I was convinced that I had to go to Canada to get that help. I had no plan but was positive that all I had to do was walk and soon I would be back in the Nicola Valley. Then I would find Ken and together we would come back and rescue Bob.

I walked along the ruined trench. There were bodies scattered everywhere, British, Canadian and German. At one point a wounded man called out to me for help, but I ignored him. He wasn't Bob.

Eventually, I came to a point where the trench was completely blown in by a large shell. I simply climbed out into the open and kept walking. Scenes of torn ground littered with ragged bodies and groups of running men appeared and disappeared through the swirling smoke, like the fragmented images from a broken moving-picture show. A heavily armed German soldier appeared out of the smoke and almost bowled me over. He glanced at my tattered uniform and bloodstained face, shouted something I didn't understand and pointed back the way he had come. Other Germans appeared and disappeared, heading for the battle, as well as scattered, unarmed and stunned British soldiers stumbling along in the opposite direction. Obviously, the Germans had been told to ignore surrendering soldiers, wave them back and not allow them to slow the advance.

I don't know how long I walked for, but it must have been several days because I remember walking in both daylight and darkness. I had no idea what direction I was headed in. I was just confident that whatever direction I chose would be the right one.

My memories of those days are confused and not at all coherent. They're a bunch of vivid images, but all unconnected, and set in a sea of tiredness and walking. When I was tired, I lay down and slept wherever I was — in a ditch, a field or a wood, it made no difference. Once a French woman took me into a barn and let me sleep on some bales of hay. Another time someone else, or the same woman, gave me a steaming hot bowl of stew. I ate it so fast I burned my mouth.

At some point I crossed back into British territory, but no one paid any attention to me there either. The roads were jammed either with long columns of exhausted retreating men or supply columns trying to get to the Front.

Once I was sleeping in a wood with a group of

other men when we were awoken by a man shouting, "The Germans have broken through. They'll be here within the hour." My companions panicked and rushed away. I got up and kept walking.

Another time I stumbled into a headquarters unit. Men were busy shoving documents into roaring fires and staff officers were piling into fancy automobiles. One officer stayed behind and tried to organize us to dig in at the edge of the wood, but as soon as he was out of sight I simply walked away.

After a while I left the crowded roads and headed across country. I met fewer soldiers and more French people. They were all women and children, working the farms as best they could with their husbands and older sons either serving in the army or already dead. For the most part they helped me, offering food and somewhere to sleep, but some chased me away, waving brooms and yelling curses I couldn't understand.

The country gradually became more heavily wooded and I began to think that I must be getting close to Ontario, where I had seen vast forests from the train windows on my journey to Halifax.

One morning I was woken up by a hand roughly shaking my shoulder. Two men stood over me.

One was wearing a faded British uniform and the other a French coat.

"Who're you?" the Englishman asked in a broad accent.

"My name's Allan McBride," I answered.

"And what're you doin' 'ere?"

"I'm going to Canada," I said. "I have to get help for my friend Bob."

"Oh God!" the Englishman exclaimed. "Another loony. That's all we need. "'Arry'll be thrilled."

He put his hand under my arm and helped me to my feet. "Come on, son. Let's go and meet the rest of the blokes."

"I have to go to Canada," I repeated.

"That's okay. It's on the way."

Arm in arm we walked through the forest. Walking to Canada on my own had been very difficult. I felt ridiculously happy to have someone to help me.

Chapter 10
Deserter
North of Béthune, Spring 1918

"Is this Ontario?" I asked when we arrived at a clearing in the woods.

"Yeah," my escort replied. "This is Ontario. Now you just wait 'ere while I fetch 'Arry."

As the soldier walked away, I looked around with interest. I had only ever seen Ontario from a train, so I figured it was good to be able to spend some time there.

The camp was a rough copy of an army camp. Several army-issue tents were spread between the trees. Rations, ammunition boxes, weapons and equipment were scattered about. Over to one side sat a Triumph Model H Roadster motorcycle and sidecar with a set of army-issue goggles slung carelessly over the handlebars. Everything was military issue, but the camp had none of the order and tidiness of a regular camp. About a dozen men either stood around smoking or sat by small fires. Most wore some semblance of a British uniform, but I spotted two Frenchmen and one

German. This was a bit confusing. I knew that the Frenchmen were probably from the neighbouring province of Quebec, but the German? Then I remembered that there were a lot of German immigrants in Ontario. Hadn't I read somewhere that a town near Toronto had changed its name from Berlin to Kitchener? I felt pleased that I had worked the problem out.

As I stood, looking about, a man approached. He was dressed in the uniform of a full major, but his tunic buttons were undone and a cigarette hung from his mouth. He looked familiar. Instinctively, I straightened and saluted. Instead of returning my salute, the man smiled.

"We don't salute here," he said. "Don't you remember me?"

I struggled to place the face and voice but had no luck. I shook my head helplessly.

"Last fall," the man said. "At Etaples. The mutiny."

Then it came to me. Harry Sommerfield. I stepped back. "You're the coward that started the riot," I said.

Sommerfield laughed. "I didn't start anything, although I did try to finish it."

"You were a private soldier," I said, staring at his uniform. "They made you an officer?"

"I made myself what I am," Sommerfield replied. "What's your name?"

"Allan McBride."

"Well, Allan, do you have any idea where you are and what's going on here?"

"I'm in Ontario," I said, a little uncertainly, "and this is — " I hesitated " — a training camp?"

"Okay, we'll call it Ontario to keep it simple, but this isn't a training camp. This here — " Sommerfield swung his arm wide to encompass the camp " — is a group of sane men who've decided that they've had enough of this war's insanity."

"Deserters!" I said in sudden realization. I turned away. "I have to go. I'm almost home and I have to get help for Bob."

Sommerfield stepped round to block my way. "Who's Bob?" he asked. "Is he in the woods here too?"

"No," I said. "He's back in the trench at Arras. There was a big attack and he was buried. I have to go home and get help for him."

"Home's a long way," Sommerfield said. "It'll take a long time to get there and get back with help. Wouldn't it be better for Bob if I helped?"

I nodded slowly. It made sense. I had been focused on going home for help and never thought of help being closer at hand.

"Why don't you go and rest while I get some things together to help Bob. When I'm ready, I'll wake you up and we can go and help him. You must be tired."

I felt a huge sense of relief. Someone else was going to help, and I didn't have to do everything on my own. It was as if Sommerfield had lifted a vast weight from my shoulders. Suddenly I felt utterly spent.

"I would like that," I said, gratefully.

"Excellent." Sommerfield took my arm and led me over to a nearby tent. "You climb in there and have a rest. I'll organize everything."

"Thank you."

I ducked into the tent, spotted a pile of blankets and curled up in a ball in the middle of them. It was like a nest and I felt safe for the first time in ages. Maybe Sommerfield wasn't so bad after all.

I just had time to hear Sommerfield say to someone, "Keep an eye on him," before blackness overwhelmed me.

When I came to, Sommerfield was sitting in the tent doorway looking at me. "Good morning," he said with a smile.

For a moment I had no idea where I was, but I felt strangely calm and, for the first time I could remember, I didn't feel exhausted. Then gradually things began to come back to me. There was something I had to do. I sat up.

"How long was I asleep?" I asked, rubbing my eyes.

"Almost three days," Sommerfield said.

"Three days!"

"I think you were sick. You had a fever."

"You should have woken me."

"I tried, but a howitzer going off in your ear wouldn't have brought you back. Besides, you needed the rest."

"But there's something I have to do. I'm going to Canada to get help for Bob." Even as I said it, I knew it was crazy. An image of Bob's blue, dead face, half buried in dirt, flashed into my mind. "He's dead," I said.

Sommerfield nodded. "And this isn't Ontario."

I suddenly saw myself hitting Bob and him falling onto the duckboards on the bottom of the trench. "I killed him." My guilt returned to weigh me down. "I hit him. I was scared and running away. He tried to stop me and I hit him. I knocked him down. Then the shell exploded. He was buried and I couldn't dig him out in time. If he hadn't been on the ground — "

I couldn't stop the tears. They flooded out as I collapsed back onto the blankets. I wept for Bob suffocating in the collapsed trench; for Mac-Taggart, decapitated by the shell; for Ken trying to kill himself because he couldn't face it all anymore; and for myself, destined to always be alone and see my friends killed around me. Eventually I cried myself out and fell back asleep.

When I woke it was dark. I could hear voices outside the tent and see the flicker of campfires. I lay for a long time thinking about my situation. It looked bleak. My past was gone. Dead with Ken, MacTaggart and Bob. My present and future were a mystery.

At last the smell of food cooking made me realize how hungry I was and drew me out of the tent. Sommerfield and the two men who had found me were sitting on logs round a small fire, where a black cast iron pot hung.

"Come on over and get something to eat," Sommerfield said when he saw me. "You must be hungry."

I edged over to the fire and sat down, not wanting to talk to anyone but salivating madly at the smell. Sommerfield took a tin plate, a spoon and a large hunk of French bread, ladled out some stew and passed it over to me. I can't remember what the stew tasted like, only that it was the best thing I had ever eaten. I finished three plate-fuls, wiped the last of the bread around the plate and looked up. Sommerfield was sitting across the fire, smiling. No one had spoken while I was eating.

Physically I felt better than I had in a long time, but my mind was cluttered with contradictions. On the one hand, I was rested, fed and apparently dream free. I had got over the insane idea of walk-ing to Canada and realized that there was nothing I could do for Bob. I almost felt relaxed.

On the other hand, I was bewildered by what had happened, scared by my madness and wor-ried about what was going to happen next. I also felt appallingly alone and had to fight to hold back tears whenever any of my dead friends and col-leagues popped into my mind.

"What day is it?" I asked Sommerfield.

"Monday," he replied.

"It can't be. The attack was on March twenty-first, which was a Thursday. If this is Monday, it doesn't leave enough time for me to get here, wherever here is."

Sommerfield and the other men exchanged glances. "Today is Easter Monday, April first. Pete and Marcel here — " Sommerfield indicated the other two men " — found you wandering in the woods three days ago."

I stared at Sommerfield, struggling to comprehend. Could the attack that had killed MacTaggart and Bob and driven me to mad flight really have been eleven days ago? That meant that there was a gap in my life of more than a week when I had wandered aimlessly and could remember only fragmentary images.

"You were shell-shocked," Sommerfield said, gently. "It's not uncommon to lose track of time. What's more remarkable is that you wandered around for so long without being picked up, but then I suppose the army's got more on its mind right now than a solitary lost soldier."

"What's happened?" I asked.

"Nous sommes finis," the soldier I assumed was Marcel grunted.

"My French companion is correct," Sommerfield said. "The attack on the twenty-first broke through almost everywhere and the Germans have been moving forward ever since. From what I've heard, they've advanced more than forty miles and stand at the gates of Amiens. If Amiens falls, the British and French armies will be split apart and the British will have to retreat to the coast. It's chaos south of here. The Germans have taken thousands of prisoners and entire regiments have disappeared. The roads are packed with refugees, the remnants of defeated units and more than a few lost souls like yourself. It's the end of the war."

Marcel stood up, spat loudly and walked away.

"Marcel is not taking the defeat of his country very well," Sommerfield said, "but it's the only way we'll have peace."

I sat and stared into the flames. Was the war really almost over? I was devastated that the Germans were going to win, but a part of me was elated — I was going to survive.

I stood up and looked over at the surrounding woods. "I have to get back to my unit . . . " I said uncertainly. The camp looked warm and inviting, the trees dark and threatening.

The soldier called Pete barked a short laugh. "Stupid bloody fool," he said. "'E survives the Germans trying to kill 'im and now 'e wants 'is own side to do the job for 'im."

"The point that Pete is rather crudely making," Sommerfield explained, "is that, like the rest of us here, you're a deserter now. You deserted your unit in the middle of a battle. You've only been lightly wounded, but you've been absent for almost two weeks while your army has been beaten senseless and lost the war. What do you think they'll do when you waltz in and say, 'Sorry I left my post, gents, but I'm back now.'?"

"I didn't know what I was doing. I was confused. I was sick. You said yourself I had a fever."

Pete snorted. "On the contrary, mate. You *did* know what you were doin' then. It's now you're confused."

"Look," Sommerfield said calmly, "whatever reasons you had for doing what you did, the army will only look at it one way: You deserted in the face of the enemy. For that they will court martial you, find you guilty, tie you to a post and shoot you. Believe me, they've done it before and they'll do it again, in all probability a matter of days after you give yourself up. They even shoot officers for doing what you did. What chance does a private have?"

What Sommerfield was saying stunned me. I knew that you could be shot for desertion, but it was not something that would ever happen to me. Only cowards deserted and they deserved to be shot. I hadn't deserted. I hadn't known what I was doing. But Sommerfield was right — that's not the way the army would see it. To them I *was* a deserter.

"What can I do?" I asked, sitting back down. I could barely get the words out.

"Only one choice as far as I can see," Sommerfield said. "Nothing's going to stop the Germans. As soon as they reach the coast, Britain and France are going to have to make peace.

"Oh, there'll be lots of shouting and a big peace conference. Some money and some land will change hands and everyone will try and claim that they did well out of it. There'll be a few years for everyone to lick their wounds and build up their armies." He spat into the fire. "And then it'll all happen again."

"But that means that we'll have fought for four years for nothing."

"For the average man it always was for nothing. What did you or I ever stand to gain from this war? If we were lucky, we'd stay alive. The only people who profit from war are the businessmen who make the guns, shells, bombs, uniforms and all the rest of the paraphernalia an army needs. They're making fortunes and you don't see a single one of them risking his life in the mud. The worker — whether he's British, French, Canadian, German or, now, American — is fighting to put money in some fat slug's pocket in London, Paris, Toronto or Berlin."

"Like the bloody Ross rifle," Pete muttered.

Sommerfield caught my questioning look and

said, "You weren't out here at the beginning, but the Canadians in 1915 and '16 were given Ross rifles instead of the British Enfields. The government wanted the contract to go to a Canadian company so their cronies could profit. Trouble was, the rifle didn't work. It jammed when the least bit of dirt got in it, the bayonet tended to fall off and, if you weren't really careful assembling it, the bolt flew back and took the side of your head off when you fired it. Everyone hated it. At Ypres in 1915, the first thing you did when you got out of the trench was find a dead Brit and take his rifle.

"Canadian boys died because of the Ross rifle, but would the government stop issuing it? No. Good old Sir Charles Ross was making a packet and he had friends in high places. What did it matter if the rifle was killing a few young soldiers? Eventually, General Haig had to order the Canadians to issue us with Enfields."

If Sommerfield had told me this story last summer, I'd have shouted him down as a liar. Now I was angry, but my anger was at Ross and the others, not Sommerfield.

"Anyway," he went on, "you stick here with us. In a few weeks it'll all be over and we can find a way to go home."

I stared into the flames. What should I do? In

my mind I wasn't a deserter, but if I chose to stay here, I would be. If I didn't stay here I would have to give myself up, and I would probably be shot for being the thing I was giving myself up to prove I *wasn't*. It was an impossible choice.

"How long have you been here?" I asked.

"Here," Sommerfield said, "only a few weeks. We have to keep moving around. If we stay in one place too long, the Red Caps find us. But if you mean how long since we left the army, it varies. I've been on the run for near eighteen months now, Marcel since the French mutinies last summer and Pete came with me from Etaples. But a couple of boys, like yourself, have drifted in over the past few days."

"I saw a German uniform."

"That would be Horst. Before the war he was a waiter in some fancy restaurant in London. Speaks better English than Pete here. He was captured over the winter but managed to escape when he was being taken back. Luckily he ran into us."

"How do you survive? Doesn't the army hunt you down?"

"They try, but it's not easy. This is a big country, there are a lot of woods and the army's got other things for its soldiers to do. On top of that, they can't officially admit that we exist. Can you

139

imagine what the papers back home would make of groups — we're not the only one, by the way — of disaffected soldiers who have simply walked away from the war, living free in the countryside. It wouldn't look good, and the more men they involve in hunting us, the more chance there is that the story will get out. As long as we don't make too much trouble, it's better for them to leave us be.

"We have to be careful. Occasionally, if we stay in one place too long, they'll send a squad of Red Caps to sweep the area, but never very many and they're fairly easy to avoid."

"Where do you get food, clothes, tents?"

"That's the easy part," Sommerfield smiled. "You see, we don't exist, so if an officer — " he ran his hand down his major's uniform " — walks into a supply depot with a convincing piece of paper requisitioning a dozen tents and rations for a company on a training exercise, no one questions it. And we get quite a bit of help from the French. Almost every family has lost someone — a son, brother or father — at Verdun, and many of them are sympathetic to us. There's even some Australians hiding out where no man's land is wide enough."

The sheer nerve of what Sommerfield said they were doing left me speechless. What he was telling me was that there were scores, perhaps hundreds, of deserters living behind and between the lines, stealing and scrounging what they needed and taking no part in the war.

"So, young Allan McBride," Sommerfield went on, "as I see it, you've got two choices. Give your-self up and let them shoot you, or stay with us and wait out the few weeks until the war ends and we can all go home."

I understood all the words Sommerfield said, but putting them together into a coherent whole seemed beyond my grasp. I felt emotionally drained and incapable of making a rational deci-sion. What should I do?

On top of everything else, I felt unbearably lonely. Ken, someone in my life as important as my father, and the only person who understood what I was going through and could give me advice, was gone. Probably dead. My hands began to shake at the pros-pect of having to make my mind up on my own.

I looked up and met Sommerfield's eyes. A smile was playing around the corners. His face was open, relaxed and friendly. I felt a surge of gratitude for this man who was prepared to help me. He would take the burden of responsibility off my shoulders. I *wasn't* alone.

"I'll stay," I said.

Chapter 11
A Plan
North of Amiens, August 10, 1918

"Per'aps there'll be a good-lookin' daughter."

I wasn't looking at Pete but I could hear the leer in his voice. We were lying at the edge of a wood, gazing down at a cluster of stone farm buildings, waiting for dusk.

"We're here to buy some *food*," I said. The man disgusted me. I would have had nothing to do with him except that Sommerfield had sent us both out to a farm to try and get some fresh food for the camp.

I had been with Sommerfield's group long enough that there was no way I could ever claim I wasn't a deserter now. The war hadn't ended in the weeks after the March attack. The German advance had ground to a halt outside Amiens. They had launched other offensives, in the south against the French — who hadn't collapsed as Sommerfield had predicted — and near Ypres. All had been successful at first, but petered out as the attackers outran their heavy artillery and suffered from exhaustion. The war was sinking back into the hopeless, bloody stalemate of the past four years.

Physically, I felt better than when I had arrived at Sommerfield's camp, and the uncontrollable shaking in my hands had eased. However, I was utterly worn out and miserable. I awoke screaming in the dark less frequently now and the nightmares were less hideous, but I hadn't rested a complete night in months. Sudden fits of paralyzing anxiety would overwhelm me, leaving me incapable of making the simplest decision, and feeling as weak as a kitten.

I felt trapped. My choices were limited by my decision in April — or was it Sommerfield's decision? — to stay with the deserters. I couldn't escape and I had no control over what happened to me. At times I tried to figure out how I might rejoin my unit, but every attempt I could imagine to return to the world I had known, led to one thing — execution as a deserter. There were times when anxiety and depression overwhelmed me and execution seemed like a tempting option, but mostly I just kept on surviving from day to day.

Life on the run with Sommerfield and the others had been straightforward enough. We moved frequently and far, and we had even been back up to the coast by Etaples, where Sommerfield had been living when I first met him. Attempts to capture us had been half-hearted, and food and supplies were easy to get, either by stealing or bartering.

The membership of the group had changed over the months. Marcel and the other Frenchman had become fed up with so many English and gone off to try and make it home, and Horst, the solitary German, had been killed when he ran into a party of British soldiers after we had split up for a move. Sommerfield's only comment was that it served him right for insisting that he stay in his German uniform. Apart from them, a few others had drifted away, but they had been replaced by occasional newcomers. Our numbers stayed constant at around a dozen. At the moment, Sommerfield and I were the only Canadians. The rest were a mixture of Irish, Scots, Australians and English. They were a rough bunch for the most part and I had nothing in common with their crude humour and violent ways. Fights were frequent in the camp on the nights when someone managed to steal some liquor.

The only person I could talk to was Sommerfield. I think he saw me as someone he could mould to his ideas, unlike the rest of the men, who seemed only interested in drinking and fighting. In any case, Sommerfield took me under his wing and always had a sympathetic word when I went to him with one of my worries. In a strange way, in this outlandish world I was not a part of, he had taken the place of Ken, and I needed him. The mere thought of leaving the group, being on my own and having to make my own decisions, frightened me almost as much as the possibility of being shot as a deserter.

Many nights I lay awake, wallowing in guilt. I felt like a coward for living comfortably while others were fighting, and I was saddened that my parents probably thought I was dead and there was no way I could tell them I wasn't. On top of everything else, Bob kept turning up in my recurring nightmares.

In them, he stood, pale and dead, about 10 feet from me, staring. He never said anything, even though I asked him why he was there. But I knew. He was accusing me. Deep down, I was certain that his death was my stupid fault. If I hadn't panicked like a coward and tried to run away, he wouldn't have tried to stop me, I wouldn't have knocked him down and the explosion wouldn't have buried and suffocated him. I had killed Bob as surely as if I had shot him myself.

Every night I would wake with a start in a cold sweat, too terrified to go back to sleep. Exhaustion overwhelmed me and everything seemed black. Sometimes I thought that my only future was to keep running until I was captured and shot.

I sank deeper and deeper into depression and avoided the others as much as possible, but sometimes, as tonight, we were thrust together.

"Come on, let's go." Pete stood and slung his rifle over his shoulder. "It's dark enough now." He was the roughest of the group. Sommerfield had told me he had been in prison before the war, and I suspected that he regarded the war as a great opportunity to get what he could for himself.

We hurried across the fields, keeping close to the edges. It was a beautiful evening, the air fresh and rich with the smell of freshly cut hay and the sound of birdsong. The clouds turning red in the western sky made me think fondly of sunsets over the Nicola Valley.

We crossed the yard behind a farmhouse and knocked on the heavy wooden door. It was opened by a middle-aged woman dressed in a coarse woollen skirt and blouse and wiping her hands on a stained apron. She was short but powerfully built, probably from a lifetime of working on the farm.

Her face was deeply lined, yet she looked us up and down and smiled a welcome.

In halting, schoolboy French, and gestures, I explained that we were heading for our unit and had been delayed by an airplane attack. We were hungry and wondered if we could exchange some equipment — I had a roll of blankets, clothing and cloth — for some eggs and a few slices of ham, or perhaps a goose that we could take back to our comrades.

It was a weak story and I doubt if she believed us, but she invited us in, sat us at a rough wooden table and fed us a thin stew and some weak wine. Two small boys, about nine and twelve, sat in a huddle by the fireplace and watched us, wide-eyed. On the mantle I noticed three photographs, two of young, smiling soldiers and one of an older man who stared suspiciously at the camera. All three photographs were draped with black ribbons.

The woman saw me looking and went over and touched each photo in turn. "*Mon mari, Pierre,*" she said. "*Nos fils . . .* our sons, *Antoine et Honoré. Tous tués . . .* " She hesitated uncertainly.

"All killed?" I asked.

"*Oui,* all killed. *Pierre et Antoine à Verdun et Honoré sur le Chemin des Dames.*" She stared for a long moment at the pictures. Was this how my parents felt back home, mourning their dead son? I swallowed back my own sadness, but before I could think of anything to say, I felt Pete tugging at my sleeve. "Let's get a goose and shove off," he said. "I 'eard noises in the barn."

"You go and get one," I said, annoyed at Pete's manner. "I'll do the bargaining."

Pete stomped off and I unrolled my bundle of supplies. I didn't bargain hard, simply placing everything on the table and asking what we could get for it. We agreed on two geese and the woman brought a tray of eggs from the kitchen. "English?" she asked.

"No. Canadian."

Her face brightened. *"Ah, oui, Canadien. Vous avez attaqué les Boches à Amiens."* Her brow wrinkled in concentration. *"Deux jours . . .* two days — " she waved her arm to the side " — past."

"Two days ago?" I asked. "Who attacked the Germans at Amiens two days ago? The Canadians?"

"Oui! Oui!" she exclaimed. *"Les Canadiens ont cassé les Boches."*

"Broke? The Canadians *broke* the Germans?"

"Oui. Ils ont avancé de treize kilomètres." She made hurried running motions with her fingers.

I made a quick calculation. "Eight miles! That's

impossible. No one has ever advanced that far in one day."

"*Oui*," she nodded vigorously. "*Un moment.*" Clutching her apron in front of her, she scuttled through to the kitchen and returned holding a newspaper. She thrust it at me. I couldn't understand the details but there was no doubting the main message. Huge headlines blared the news that the German lines had collapsed, that huge advances into open country had been made and that it was the Canadians who were leading the attack.

"*C'est magnifique, non? Les Boches sont finis.*"

I didn't know what to say. Could it be true? Had the Canadians really won a great victory? Was the war going to end?

"I have to show this to Pete," I said, standing up, waving the newspaper and pointing to the door. The woman nodded.

I had barely stepped outside when I heard a scream from the barn. Dropping the paper, I ran across the yard. Just inside the barn door, there was a girl lying on a pile of straw, wide-eyed and gasping. She could have been no more than fifteen. A red mark was deepening above her left eye. Pete stood over her, glaring.

"No!" I yelled. I rushed at Pete. He was broader

and stronger than me, and he knew how to use his fists, but my first rush took him by surprise. We crashed into the wall and onto the floor.

We struggled for a while before Pete threw me off and stood up. His first punch caught me on the cheek. I managed to keep my feet and moved forward, but he grabbed my jacket in both hands and drove his forehead into my nose. I heard a loud crack as pain jolted though me. Pete brought his knee up into my groin and I collapsed in a heap, gasping and tasting the blood running from my nose.

"I'll finish with you later," Pete snarled as he drove his boot into my ribs. "Right now, I'm goin' to — "

"Don't," I said, as loud as I could manage. I tried to stand, but pain swamped me and I collapsed back, retching. I could hear the girl whimpering again.

"Tell *me* what to do, will you," Pete said, landing another kick to my ribs. "You're nothin' but a snivellin' little wretch from a godforsaken colony. I'm sick of your — "

I squinted up to see why Pete had stopped in mid-sentence. He was standing over me, staring down at the four thin tines of a pitchfork sticking out the front of his chest. A startled look crossed his face as he pawed helplessly at the two long-est ones. Blood was already soaking his uniform front. Then he looked at me. "What . . . ?" was all he managed to say before he gave an odd, gurgling gasp, coughed out a mouthful of blood and fell to the ground. When he landed, the long handle of the pitchfork stood straight out of his back. Behind it stood the woman.

"*Partez!*" she said.

I struggled to my feet and stumbled out the barn door. Pain radiated from my nose right through my head. My ribs throbbed with every step, but I forced myself to continue across the fields and into the trees. As soon as I was covered by the darkness, I slumped down with my back against a gnarled oak and caught my breath. The pain in my chest eased and I gingerly felt the spots where Pete's boots had landed. They were sore, but it didn't feel as if anything was broken. My nose, however, was streaming blood, and as I dug my handkerchief out of my trouser pocket and held it to my face, I thought about how things had sud-denly changed.

Pete was dead. That didn't bother me. In fact, I was glad I had helped save the girl from whatever he had in mind. Part of me was elated that Canada had won such a great victory. I was proud, but I also felt guilty. I should have been there. While my countrymen had been doing what no one else had managed in four years of war, I had been skulking in the woods.

I sat as the full moon, huge and bright, rose slowly into a gap between the trees. Something — an owl, I assumed — flashed silently across its silver face. Gradually, I made up my mind. I was going back. My place was with the Canadian army, not the deserters in the woods. It was a difficult decision to make, but the time had come to choose between the person I had been when I joined up and the person I had become — between Ken and Sommerfield. Even if Ken was now only a memory, I owed it to him to do the honourable thing, regardless of the consequences. If I didn't, Ken's ghost would always haunt me. He had gone through much worse than I had and he hadn't deserted. He had tried to keep going, to fulfil his responsibility to his men, right up until the strain had become too much and he had completely broken down. Even then, that night when he had stood up in the harsh glare of the German flare, his answer had been to die rather than leave.

Sommerfield's answer was always the easy one. He had taken the safest option and thought only of himself. There had to be more to life than that. Ken knew it and now so did I. I wasn't going to be seduced by Sommerfield any longer. Tomorrow I would leave the camp, walk to Amiens and give myself up to the first Canadian patrol I came across.

The journey back to the camp took hours. The night was warm and the full moon gave me some light through the trees. At times it was all I could manage to crawl forward, and every movement was agony. My nose wouldn't stop bleeding and my head throbbed, but my decision, and a vague sense that Ken was watching over me with approval, kept me struggling on. At last, I collapsed gratefully beside the campfire.

Sommerfield, wearing his major's uniform complete with more medal ribbons than I remembered from last time, put a field dressing on my bloody nose and attached it behind my head. He cleaned me up and gave me a stiff shot of brandy before he asked what had happened. The brandy made me choke, but its warmth revived me enough to give the group a short version of events leading to Pete's death.

"Fool," was Sommerfield's only comment on Pete's behaviour. "Get some rest," he ordered everyone. "Tomorrow at first light we move on. That woman will have every Red Cap for miles around combing these woods for us in no time. We'll split up and head northeast. We'll meet up at that old camp near Béthune."

"The woman at the farm told me something and showed me a newspaper," I said, once everyone had moved away and it was only Sommerfield and me by the fire. "The Canadians broke through at Amiens two days ago. They advanced eight miles in the first day alone."

"I know," he said. "While you were away today, I took the Triumph and paid a visit to the big camp outside Amiens. The advance is still going on. The German resistance is crumbling and thousands of prisoners have been taken."

"This attack's different, isn't it?" I asked. "This is the end of the war."

Sommerfield nodded. "I think you're right. It won't end tomorrow, but this is the year the war really *will* be over by Christmas. With the Americans here, there are enough fresh soldiers and new equipment to keep the pressure on the Germans. I saw lines of those new tank things waiting to go forward. The Gerries will only get weaker as we get stronger."

"I've made a decision," I said, steeling myself

to tell Sommerfield I was going to turn myself in. Before I had a chance to go on, he interrupted me.

"This is our chance to come out of this mess free and clear," he said. "Tomorrow, we'll let the others leave first thing, and then we'll go, but not northeast. You and I will head north to Boulogne. We'll get a boat over to England. Once there, it should be simple enough to wait out the war and then catch a boat back to Canada."

It took me a moment to understand what he was saying. "It's impossible to get on a boat. Boulogne is crawling with Red Caps. No deserter anyone has ever heard of has made it onto one of the boats to England."

"No one's had *these* before," Sommerfield said triumphantly, reaching into his uniform pocket to pull out several folded sheets of paper. He held one up. "These are blank leave forms and travel requisitions."

"Where did you get *those?*" I asked. "They're worth their weight in gold to anyone trying to get out of France. The army guards them like the crown jewels."

"I have my ways," Sommerfield said with a wink. "Actually, I've had these for some time. Just been waiting for the right moment to use them, and this is it."

"Why me?" I asked.

"We Canadians have to stick together," Sommerfield said with a laugh.

He must have seen from my expression that I didn't believe him, because he continued. "Because you can carry it off. Pete would have gone and done something stupid and got caught. The others are just a rabble, and I meant it about us Canadians sticking together. It'll look less suspicious if we're both Canadians. People might ask questions if my companion has a strong Australian accent. Besides, no one will question two wounded men, a major and a private, with all the right paperwork. You already look as if you've fought the battle of Amiens all on your own."

"But you're not wounded."

"Not yet." Sommerfield pulled his pistol out of its holster, held up his left hand and shot off his small finger. The pinkie tumbled through the air and landed 10 feet away.

He gasped and held his injured hand to his chest. A few heads poked out of tent flaps to see what the commotion was.

"It's okay, boys," Sommerfield said in a strained voice. "Pistol went off by accident. No harm done." The heads withdrew.

He replaced his pistol and proceeded to wrap a bandage around his bleeding hand.

"Do this in the trenches and you're up for a court martial, but no one will question a decorated officer — " he patted his medal ribbons " — and a brave private with his head half bandaged up. Blood's already seeping through the dressing. You look very convincing as the wounded hero. Now get some sleep. I'm going to fill out these forms so that they're nice and dry before we leave. Even on the cycle it's a long journey up to Boulogne."

He stood up, cradling his crudely bandaged hand across his chest. "Don't look so serious. We're nearly home free." He saw me looking at his hand. "And don't worry about this. I never use that finger anyway. It's a good exchange for freedom."

I stared after Sommerfield as he walked away. I almost called him back to tell him I'd decided to give myself up, but I was sore, exhausted and reeling from the events of the evening. And, if I was honest, Sommerfield's offer was tempting. It sounded so easy. Use the forms to get over to England. Slip onto a boat to Canada amid the euphoria of a victorious end to the war. In a matter of few months, I could be walking in the door back at the Nicola Valley farm and hugging my mother.

The alternative could be standing tied to a post as the bullets from a firing squad ripped into my chest.

I shuddered and cursed Sommerfield for undermining my resolve. Praying that I would feel stronger in the morning, I dragged myself over to my tent and collapsed into a bone-weary sleep.

Chapter 12
An End
North of Amiens, August 11, 1918

My first sensation as I awoke from a deep sleep was of freedom, then I realized why. My sleep had been utterly dreamless. None of the dead had visited to accuse me. Even Bob had stayed away and, although I had no rational reason to believe it, I knew he was gone for good. I felt rested for the first time in as long as I could remember. In that moment I also understood *why* I was free. I had made the right decision and knew what I had to do. Sommerfield's plan was just another easy solution. It might save my body, but it did nothing to resolve the conflict in my mind. Giving myself up was hard, but if I didn't do it, I would be burdened by guilt and shame for the rest of my life.

I crawled out of the tent and looked round. Discarded equipment lay all over but Sommerfield was the only person in sight. He was standing by the motorcycle with a leather dispatch pouch tucked under his left arm.

"Grab whatever you need and come help me. Packing up one-handed isn't as easy as I thought." He laughed shortly and turned away.

I stood up and stretched. It was a beautiful morning. The sun was sending bright shafts of light through the trees and the sky straight overhead was the colour of a robin's egg. A squirrel complained about something in a nearby tree. It was going to be hot later, but it was still cool among the trees.

"I'm not coming with you," I said.

"What?" Sommerfield asked mildly, half turning.

"I said I'm not coming with you. I'm going to Amiens to turn myself in. I was going to tell you last night."

"What do you mean?" he asked, slowly completing his turn towards me. His face was darkening with anger. "Don't be a bloody fool. I thought you were over the stupid idea of going back and getting shot."

"I have to go," I said. "It's the right thing to do."

"The right thing to do?" Sommerfield snarled and strode towards me. "What do you, a dim-witted boy who should still be at home playing with his lead soldiers, know about what's right? What's right is to stay alive in this godforsaken mess. To survive at all costs."

Sommerfield was right in front of me now, shouting in my face. I could feel his spit land on my forehead. "I need you to help me get on the boat," he yelled.

"You'll have to manage that on your own," I said, turning on my heel and striding away. "I'm going to Amiens to turn myself in."

Sommerfield caught me after two steps. His right hand grabbed my shoulder and spun me round. It was only because he had to let go of me and draw back his right fist to hit me that I had time to react. I swung wildly at him. It was a clumsy blow and wouldn't have done much damage, except that Sommerfield instinctively raised his left arm to protect himself and my punch landed square on his mutilated hand. He yelled in pain and sat down heavily.

I crossed the clearing feeling powerful and confident. I was in charge of my own life at last. I heard a voice order, "Don't move," but I ignored it. Sommerfield had no power over me now.

I had gone just a little way into the trees when the figure stepped out in front of me. "It's a long way to Amiens," it said.

I heard the words, but I wasn't really listening. I recognized the face not 3 feet in front of me. "Ken?" I asked. "Is that really you?"

My first reaction was that I was in a dream and this was another ghost come to haunt me. My chest tensed so much I had trouble breathing. Pain shot across my bruised ribs. My hands started twitching and I sank to my knees.

"I saw you *shot*," I managed to gasp. "You're dead."

"Almost," Ken said with a smile, "and not for want of trying, although I lost a lung and a couple of ribs, so hunting mountain sheep is not an option anymore. But we'll talk later. I think we should go back to the clearing now."

Ken helped me up and we returned the way I had come. I was confused by his sudden appearance, but glad that I had made my decision to surrender before he had arrived.

Sommerfield was sitting morosely on a stump by the ashes of the fire. His pistol was missing from its holster but he still carried the dispatch pouch containing the travel documents beneath his left arm. The grubby bandage round his hand was stained dark with blood. A sergeant and half a dozen young armed soldiers stood around the clearing.

"Looks like the rest of the birds've flown, sir,' the sergeant reported.

"Which way did the rest of the deserters go?" Ken asked.

"They're heading northeast, towards Béthune," I answered automatically.

"On foot?"

I nodded.

"And how much of a start do they have?"

"They left this morning, so it can't be that long," I said.

"Very well," Ken said. "Sergeant, leave one man with me. Take the rest of the squad and sweep to the northeast. See how many you can pick up. Bring them back here."

"Right you are, sir." The sergeant delegated one man, a very young looking private, to stay, and rapidly organized the others into a widely-spaced line that set off at a brisk pace through the trees.

When we couldn't hear them any more, Ken sat us down around the dead fire. The private sat to my left, his rifle held nervously across his knees. Ken sat to my right, on the opposite side from Sommerfield. A faint smile played on his face.

I was still in shock, but questions were beginning to flood my mind. "What happened? Were you trying to kill yourself when you stood up back there in no man's land? If you only have one lung why aren't you at home? What are you doing here?" I asked.

"Slow down. I'll tell you what I can." Ken paused for a moment before launching into his story. "Yes, I was trying to kill myself. I couldn't see any other way out. I was a complete wreck — not sleeping, plagued by dreams, sinking deeper into black depression and spending every spare moment trying to concoct mad schemes that would get me home. Fortunately, I was still sane enough to see that they wouldn't work, but I *was* trapped. The responsibility I felt for all the men in the Company weighed heavy and I simply couldn't face watching any more of them die. The thought of the coming German attack was just too much to bear."

"Touching," Sommerfield remarked, frowning.

Ken flashed him a look and continued. "When I was caught by that flare on the raid, it suddenly struck me how easy it would be to simply stand up and not have to go through all the rest. So I did. I remember waking up in a hospital bed somewhere. I had just dreamed that I was dead and when I realized that I was still alive, I felt horribly disappointed. But I was lucky."

Ken absent-mindedly rubbed the side of his chest where I had seen the bullet exit wound, before he continued. "A doctor in London realized that I had more wrong with me than a bullet through the chest. He arranged to have me transferred to Craiglockhart, a place up in Scotland where there was a Doctor Rivers who was working with shell-shocked officers. The man was a wonder. He actually understood.

"As the weeks passed, my dreams and fears grew less. By the summer, I was ready to leave Craiglockhart. I wasn't cured — I doubt I ever will be — but I could function."

Ken smiled. He looked more relaxed than I remembered seeing him since before he went off to war.

"Rivers wanted me discharged from the army, but I was desperate to return to France. I felt guilty that I had let my men — and you, Allan — down. We compromised. I could come back to France, but only for duty behind the front lines. They gave me the job of organizing squads of men on sweeps of the countryside to pick up deserters. We've had a certain amount of luck, but there aren't many men available for this work.

"In any case, I'd heard reports of a group living in these woods and I was setting up a sweep when word arrived last night that a French woman had killed a British deserter.

"I guessed that the rest of the group would probably leave after what had happened, so we moved quickly. We began the sweep while it was still dark. We would have missed you two if you'd left with the others."

"Lucky us," Sommerfield muttered.

"Keep your mouth shut," Ken ordered.

"Yes, sir," Sommerfield replied, his right hand rising to his forehead in an insolent, mock salute.

"I was on my way to Amiens to give myself up," I said, so quietly that Ken had to lean forward to hear me.

"I know you were," Ken said. "I heard you tell Sommerfield that's what you were going to do. I guess I saved you a walk.

"I could hardly believe it when I saw you in the clearing," Ken went on. "I knew you'd been reported missing, but that could have meant you were dead, a prisoner, or a deserter. I heard it was utter chaos in those first days of the German attack. I thought being a deserter was a possibility because I had seen some symptoms in you that I recognized — the occasional twitch, the inability to sleep, the faraway look in the eyes. I knew if you were a deserter it was because you were sick, like I was. You don't have to worry any more, Allan. I'll get you some help."

I felt my throat tighten. Ken, the hero of my childhood, the man who had saved my life and the one I had followed into the war, was back to help me again.

The pistol shot was deafening. Out of the corner of my eye, I saw the young private cartwheel backwards as a red halo sprayed from his head. His rifle spun to the ground at my feet.

Ken reached for his holster, but Sommerfield stopped him. "I wouldn't do that." He was sitting calmly, pointing a pistol across the firepit at Ken. He must have had it hidden in the dispatch case.

Ken relaxed and let his hand fall back on his lap. "You won't get away with this," he said. "The rest of the squad will have heard the shot. They'll be back soon."

"True," Sommerfield said, "but on foot. I doubt they can outrun a motorcycle. Still, you have a point. I should hurry. Allan, get the private's rifle and come over here."

I hesitated, confused by the speed of events and still trying to make sense of what was happening. "I — I don't know," I stammered.

"Look," Sommerfield said. "I'll forget what you said earlier. Like your friend here says, you're sick. But don't believe what he told you. Do you honestly think anyone will listen to him? He's still alive because he tried to kill himself and because he's an officer. You're a soldier who ran away in the middle of a battle. They'll shoot you as certainly as the sun will come up tomorrow. You've

167

got one chance to get out of this mess free, and that's to come with me now."

I looked at Ken. He was smiling. It was a friendly, comforting expression. It was the smile I had seen after I had fallen on the sheep-hunting trip. The smile I had seen as he fashioned a makeshift splint and carried me down the mountain ahead of the snowstorm.

I looked over at Sommerfield. He was smiling as well, but it was the smile of a predator.

"What will you do with him if I come with you?" I asked, jerking my thumb at Ken. If I could keep Sommerfield talking, there might be time for the sergeant and his men to return.

"We'll leave him here," Sommerfield replied. His smile broadened, but his eyes remained cold.

I knew what that smile meant. "I don't want him hurt."

"Of course not. It won't hurt. Now hurry up, we need to go." Sommerfield stood up.

I bent down and picked up the soldier's rifle. Standing up, I slipped the safety catch off and, hoping the dead man had put a bullet in the chamber, pointed the rifle across the firepit.

Sommerfield looked puzzled. "What in blazes are you doing?"

"Like I said, I'm not coming with you," I

hissed. "You get on your cycle and go, but we're staying here."

"Don't be stupid, Allan. This officer — " Sommerfield spat the word out " — can't save your life. I can. The plan will work if we leave here together, but we have to leave *now*."

I felt beads of sweat forming on my neck and running down under my uniform collar. The rifle barrel wavered, but then it steadied. I had made my decision — Sommerfield or Ken. All I had to do was stick with it.

"Put the pistol down," I ordered, surprised at the firmness in my voice. "Get on your cycle and leave."

Sommerfield wouldn't give up. "We're comrades, Allan," he said, his smile returning. "We've both been through hell and survived. I've looked after you and helped you for months. Now we have a chance to get out forever. Are you going to let this stuck-up officer stand in our way? Give me the rifle and we'll go home."

"This officer's my friend," I said. "You are not. You just want someone to make your escape easier."

Sommerfield's smile vanished and he let out a long sigh. The pistol in his right hand began to swing towards me. It seemed to be happening in

169

slow motion and I had time to think quite clearly: *He's going to kill me.* I looked down the barrel of Sommerfield's pistol and squeezed the trigger.

I wasn't holding the rifle properly and the kick knocked me a step backwards. That's what saved my life. I heard a whine as the pistol bullet passed an inch away from my right ear. I regained my balance, worked the rifle bolt to eject the old cartridge and pointed the weapon back at Sommerfield.

There was no need. He stood, staring at me, the pistol hanging from his limp right arm. A dark stain was growing on the left side of his chest, just below his row of fake medal ribbons.

"You shot me," Sommerfield said with great effort. He tried to say more but his lips just moved silently. He slowly sank down against one of the stumps.

Ken stepped over and took the pistol from Sommerfield's grasp. Then he came back and prised the rifle out of my grip.

"He's dead," Ken said. "You saved my life."

I knew I had. I knew Sommerfield was going to kill both of us, but that didn't make me feel good about killing him.

Ken put his arm around my shoulder and I collapsed against him. I didn't cry. I felt completely empty, drained of every emotion except relief that it was finally over.

The sergeant, returning with his men and some of the deserters, found us that way, sitting by the fire-pit with the dead private and Sommerfield. Ken had said nothing in the time we were waiting; he was simply my friend comforting me. But now he resumed his role of officer, detailing men to guard the prisoners and search the camp for weapons, and sending a runner back to headquarters with a request for stretcher bearers and Red Caps.

I sat and watched everything as if I were at a moving picture theatre running a Charlie Chaplin film. My life up to that point seemed like a ser-ies of dreams — growing up in the Nicola Val-ley . . . the war . . . living as a deserter. Only this moment appeared real, but there was a distance. Life around me went on, but I couldn't affect it. All I could do was watch.

The feeling continued into the afternoon when the Red Caps arrived, put me in with the other deserters and herded us out of the woods. Ken tried to encourage me, taking me aside and saying he would move heaven and earth to get me sent to Doctor Rivers's care at Craiglockhart. I smiled and thanked him, but I didn't care. Life could do with me as it wanted. I was through with trying to control or change things.

In the days after I shot Sommerfield, my dreams returned. They weren't as frequent as before, they didn't leave me with the same sense of growing dread, but they came often enough for me to awake screaming. The shaking only returned after a particularly bad dream, but I had trouble focussing and found myself drifting off in the middle of conversations, even ones that concerned my life and death.

At least, my guilt went away. I no longer felt responsible for Bob's death. It was sad and I still missed his cheerful personality, and I knew it was wrong of me to have hit him, but I realized that I hadn't had control over the shell that exploded on the parapet. And who can say what would have happened had Bob remained standing. It was standing up that had caused MacTaggart's death.

I didn't feel any guilt around killing Sommerfield either. He was about to kill us both. Not that I minded about me, but I was glad that I had saved Ken's life. In a strange sense it balanced things and repaid him for saving my life on the hunting trip.

Sommerfield taught me things, too — that life is not fair, and that officers are treated differently from privates, just as the rich lead very different lives from the poor. I never believed in Sommerfield's ideas of violent revolution and change, but I doubt I'll ever again see the world as the simple and uncomplicated place I once thought it to be. The problem is, I don't have very long to see the world anyway.

Epilogue

Outside Amiens, August 24, 1918

"Have you managed to get it all written down?" I ask Paul, who's been scribbling all night trying to keep up with my torrent of words.

I have almost no voice left. It's a wrench coming back from all those memories to the grubby hut in the quarry, with that bleak post set in the ground outside.

The dawn light suddenly seems very bright as the candle stub flickers.

"Yes, Allan, I think I got it all," Paul says. He finishes writing and puts down his pencil.

"Good," I reply, nodding. I'm content. "I don't suppose there's anything left to tell you, then. Will you make sure my story gets to my parents?"

"I will."

At the thought of my parents, a wave of sadness sweeps over me. I want nothing more than to go home and see them for one last time, but it's not possible.

"And will you give a copy to Lieutenant Ken Harrison?"

Paul nods.

I had half hoped that Ken would be the one to sit with me this final night. He had spoken passionately at my court martial, saying that I was shell-shocked, confused and had had no intention of deserting when I wandered away from my unit. He also told them about overhearing me telling Sommerfield that I was setting out for Amiens to give myself up.

But it had done no good. The officers had listened sympathetically, but the facts were clear — in their eyes I had deserted so I had to be condemned. Still, I'm sorry that I never had a chance to thank Ken, and it would be nice to be able to say goodbye.

"The firing squad will be here soon?" I ask.

Paul glances at his wristwatch. It's light enough to read the time without the candle. "They should have been here already," he says, looking puzzled.

"I'm glad they gave us enough time to finish the story."

The knock on the door makes Paul jump, but I sit calmly. Not much scares me anymore. The door creaks open to reveal a second officer silhouetted in the frame. "Hello, Allan," he says.

"Hello, Ken," I reply, happy that he has come.

He steps in and stands beside the table. "Your reprieve has come through," he says.

I nod as if I had been expecting it. I know I should react more, feel a surge of joy or something, but too much has happened. I feel numb. It will take time for it all to sink in, although I am glad that I will have the chance to see Mom and Dad once more.

"Word should have got to you earlier, but I wanted to tell you myself. I had to go all the way up to General Currie, and he had to talk to Haig. I like to think it was my passion and arguments, and the fact that you saved my life, that did it, but the truth is that the war continues to go well and the General Staff are more inclined to commute death sentences."

I nod again, not saying anything.

"And I have more good news. Though I cannot get you into Craiglockhart — that is for officers only — I wrote to Dr. Rivers and he has agreed to treat you privately. I have a travel pass and tickets to get you to Scotland."

"Thank you, Ken," I say. "And thank you, Paul," I add, standing and holding out my hand him. He stands and takes it.

"I'm glad it turned out well, Allan," he says.

"Well?" I repeat. "I don't know about that. At least I now have time to find out."

I walk across the room and step though the door into the sunlight. Ken follows me.

Paul stands for a moment, staring after the pair, then he turns and blows out the candle. He picks up his notebook with its pages of shorthand scrawl and gazes at it thoughtfully. Slowly he closes it and returns it to his uniform pocket. On his way out he collects his pistol from the guard. As an afterthought, he turns back and gives him the unopened bottle of whiskey.

Historical Note

Today we remember the taking of Vimy Ridge on Easter Monday, 1917, as the defining Canadian moment in the First World War. Certainly, the Canadians' storming of the heights that had defied capture by both the British and French for two years was a great achievement. More than that, the memorialization of that battle did much to cement a sense of national identity. However, in the grand strategy of the war it was a relatively minor victory in the much larger engagement that was the terrible Battle of Arras. That is another fight that should engage our attention and command our pride.

When the First World War began in the fall of 1914, Canadians and other members of the British Empire around the world rushed to volunteer. In April 1915 a Canadian division fought bravely at Ypres, preventing a breakthrough when the Germans used poison gas for the first time on the Western Front. By the fall of 1916, there were four Canadian divisions in the Canadian Corps, three of which were heavily engaged at the battle of Flers-Courcelette in

September. At Vimy, the four Canadian divisions fought together for the first time, although still under a British commanding officer, Lieutenant-General Julian Byng. In August 1917 the Canadian Corps fought for the first time under a Canadian commander, Lieutenant-General Sir Arthur Currie, at Hill 70 outside the French city of Lens. In October the Canadians returned to the same place that the 1st Canadian Division had fought in 1915 — again as a coherent unit — and fought their way to what was left of the village of Passchendaele before the winter weather mercifully ended the Third Battle of Ypres.

The Canadians learned a lot at both Vimy and Passchendaele, primarily about how to use their artillery to neutralize the German defences that had thwarted so many previous attacks. (At Vimy the Canadian guns destroyed 83 per cent of the German guns before the soldiers even left their trenches.) The Canadians practised their novel techniques and were lucky enough not to be in the front lines when the Germans launched their devastating attacks in March 1918. By the time the Germans wore themselves out, the four divisions of the Canadian Corps were a cohesive, efficient, battle-hardened unit ready to hit back.

On August 8, 1918, outside Amiens, the Canadian Corps, with the French to their south and the Australians to their north, attacked. Supported by tanks, the Canadians advanced 13 kilometres, the farthest single-day advance of any Allied attack since the first trenches were dug in 1914. The Canadians and Australians broke through the German defences into open country and began the hundred days of advance that led to the Germans seeking an armistice to end the war on November 11, 1918. General Erich Ludendorff, the German commander, called August 8 "the black day of the German army."

The victory at Vimy remains in our minds because of the taking of the ridge after so many failed attempts, but also because there is a huge, magnificent memorial sitting on top of the ridge to keep that nation-building event fresh in our minds. Passchendaele holds a place in our imaginations because of the images of the mud and the horrific conditions in which the troops were asked to fight. There is no soaring memorial dominating the checkerboard of ordered fields around Amiens, and there was no slogging through corpse-riddled mud on August 8, 1918. Admittedly, Vimy and Passchendaele made the victory at Amiens possible, but Canadians should be equally proud of what their soldiers did the day the Allies finally broke through the German lines.

In my story, Allan McBride's adventures are all based on fact. The 2nd Division served in all the places I mention, but no single unit within the Division served specifically in all the places Allan was. However, those places exist and the things that happened there really happened.

There were no Canadian units in the British front lines when the Germans broke through on March 21, 1918. I kept Allan's Company "in the action" by having some of them sent to the British lines to learn the new techniques of defence that were being developed at that time. This was a common enough occurrence and was used to give as many units as much experience as possible.

The descriptions of trench life and the fighting at Passchendaele and in March of 1918 are accurate and based on numerous published descriptions. The mutiny at Etaples is loosely based on events that happened there in September 1917. It was triggered by a Red Cap shooting and killing a Scottish soldier on the bridge, although the Australians at Etaples were already upset at the arrest in August of one of their soldiers who had shouted abuse at an officer when the water was cut off during his shower. But these were only the triggers. The underlying reasons for the mutiny at Etaples were the brutal conditions in the camp — the endless marches, harsh punishments and primitive living conditions. These conditions were seriously resented by the soldiers there, especially those who had been in battle and were returning to the Front to fight again. The soldiers hated the Red Caps, whom they saw as bullies who didn't have to fight with the regular troops. The men detested the restrictions placed on them, particularly the limits on access to the local town.

When the rioting exploded, it was mainly a violent expression of frustration by men who had had enough bullying and who knew they might well be dead in a few weeks. Most of the mutineers expressed themselves in attacking the Red Caps, burning some buildings and invading the town in search of alcohol and a good time. Their demands were simply for better conditions and more free time.

Having said that, there were political agitators in the British army who saw the recent Russian revolution and the French Army mutinies of 1917 as the beginning of a broader class war against the rich and powerful. Undoubtedly some of them were active during the mutiny, but Etaples wasn't a revolution — it was a riot.

Understandably enough, the British authorities did not want word of the mutiny at Etaples to get out and potentially cause unrest elsewhere in the army. They kept it a secret and sent the men involved to the Front at Ypres as soon as possible. It has to be said that the men who rioted for a week at Etaples went quietly to do what they saw as their duty in the mud around Passchendaele.

The character of Harry Sommerfield is inspired by a real figure named Percy Toplis. Toplis was a petty criminal who had deserted and who lived by impersonating officers. He may have been a major instigator at Etaples, but little is known for certain of his activities at that time. Toplis was ambushed and shot dead by a policeman on the evening of June 6, 1920, on a quiet country road outside Penrith in the English Lake District.

During the war, the British authorities also suppressed information about desertion, sometimes even going to the length of lying to the next of kin of men executed. Between August 4, 1914, and November 11, 1918, around 3000 British and Empire soldiers were sentenced to death, the vast majority for desertion. Three hundred and six, including twenty-five Canadians, were actually tied to posts, blindfolded and shot at dawn by their comrades. Of the Canadians, two had been convicted of murder and one of cowardice. Twenty-two were shot for desertion. No Australians were shot, since their government did not allow the British to carry out executions for desertion.

The intriguing thing when reading the stories of the 306 men who were shot is how some of the deserters among them remained at large in the French countryside for months — in at least one case almost a year. It's reasonable to assume that some of the 2700 others, whose death sentences were commuted, were also at large for a considerable time. It's also probable that some deserters, like Percy Toplis, were never captured at all.

Of course, it was not only the British Army that executed deserters. Officially, the Germans shot 48 of their own men, although the figure is almost certainly low, as most records no longer exist. The French Army shot more than 600 soldiers, many during the mutinies of 1917, where there are persistent stories of decimation. (Decimation was a process used by the Romans, in which a unit to be punished — most commonly for mutiny or desertion in battle — is lined up and officers select every tenth man in line for execution.)

For French soldiers, desertion and evading capture were easier than for the British. France was their homeland and a number of them simply went home to hide on the family farm. There are persistent but unverified stories of mixed groups of deserters living in the French countryside, which was wilder and, in wartime, more chaotic than now. If these stories are true, the men must have existed in small groups that moved around and often received help from the locals. We don't have clear details about these groups, but how else would some deserters evade capture for months in the French countryside?

Some deserters in the First World War left their units consciously, calculating their chances and planning their escape. However, most, like Allan, had no intention of deserting. They suffered from what was then called shell shock. Today they would almost certainly be diagnosed with Post Traumatic Stress Disorder (PTSD). PTSD occurs when someone experiences unbearable stress, a violent attack, a natural disaster or battle. The symptoms have been recorded, but not understood, among soldiers for at least 2500 years. These include flashbacks to the trauma, nightmares, guilt, depression, emotional numbing and memory problems. Photographs of soldiers suffering from PTSD tend to show them wide-eyed and staring into the distance, the so-called "thousand-yard stare."

Most officers and doctors in the First World War didn't recognize shell shock as a psychological condition, and considered the sufferers as malingerers or cowards. A few far-sighted doctors recognized the men's symptoms as a genuine problem and attempted to treat it. The most famous of these was Dr. W. H. R. Rivers, who, along with several colleagues, worked with officers (including the poets Wilfred Owen and Siegfried Sassoon) at Craiglockhart Hospital in Edinburgh, Scotland.

It seems particularly harsh that, through ignorance, hundreds of young men were executed simply because they were ill. On December 11, 2001, Canada's Veterans Affairs Minister rose in the House of Commons in Ottawa to read the names of the 23 Canadians shot for desertion or cowardice into the Parliamentary Record and the Book of Remembrance. Minister Ron J. Duhamel said: "Those who go to war at the request of their nation do not know the fate that lies in store for them. This was a war of such overwhelming sound, fury and unrelenting horror that few combatants could remain unaffected. While we cannot relive those awful years of a nation at peril in total war, and although the culture of that time is subsequently too distant for us to comprehend fully, we can give these twenty-three soldiers a dignity that is their due, and provide closure to their families."

In 2006 the British Government pardoned all of the British and Commonwealth soldiers shot for desertion in the First World War.

James Cleland Richardson, twenty, whose courageous piping in the face of intense enemy fire inspired Canadian troops to storm German positions during the Battle of the Somme.

Members of a French Canadian infantry battalion repair trenches with sandbags. Duckboards at the bottom of the trenches kept the soldiers out of some of the mud and water.

Massive howitzers set up a barrage across the enemy lines, September 1916.

Soldiers in a shell hole hold the line during the Battle of Passchendaele.

Canadian troops go over the top.

Wounded Canadian soldiers are taken to an aid post during the Battle of Passchendaele.

Shocked and wounded soldiers are treated in a churchyard which was being used as a dressing station, July 1916.

ATTESTATION PAPER.

No. 67882

Folio. D Co

CANADIAN OVER-SEAS EXPEDITIONARY FORCE.

QUESTIONS TO BE PUT BEFORE ATTESTATION.

1. What is your name? *Elsworth Young*
2. In what Town, Township or Parish, and in what Country were you born? *Halifax City*
3. What is the name of your next-of-kin? *Mrs Emma Young*
4. What is the address of your next-of-kin? *Glace Bay CB*
5. What is the date of your birth? *June 22 1895*
6. What is your Trade or Calling? *Miner*
7. Are you married? *No*
8. Are you willing to be vaccinated or re-vaccinated? *Yes*
9. Do you now belong to the Active Militia? *No*
10. Have you ever served in any Military Force? *No*
    If so, state particulars of former Service.
11. Do you understand the nature and terms of your engagement? *Yes*
12. Are you willing to be attested to serve in the CANADIAN OVER-SEAS EXPEDITIONARY FORCE? *Yes*

Elsworth Young (Signature of Man).
J H Tupper Stutt (Signature of Witness).

DECLARATION TO BE MADE BY MAN ON ATTESTATION.

I, *Elsworth Young*, do solemnly declare that the above answers made by me to the above questions are true, and that I am willing to fulfil the engagements by me now made, and I hereby engage and agree to serve in the Canadian Over-Seas Expeditionary Force, and to be attached to any arm of the service therein, for the term of one year, or during the war now existing between Great Britain and Germany should that war last longer than one year, and for six months after the termination of that war provided His Majesty should so long require my services, or until legally discharged.

Date *November 26* 191 *Elsworth Young* (Signature of Recruit)
J H Tupper Stutt (Signature of Witness)

OATH TO BE TAKEN BY MAN ON ATTESTATION.

I, *Elsworth Young*, do make Oath, that I will be faithful and bear true Allegiance to His Majesty King George the Fifth, His Heirs and Successors, and that I will as in duty bound honestly and faithfully defend His Majesty, His Heirs and Successors, in Person, Crown and Dignity, against all enemies, and will observe and obey all orders of His Majesty, His Heirs and Successors, and of all the Generals and Officers set over me. So help me God.

Elsworth Young (Signature of Recruit)
Date *November 26* 191 *J H Tupper Stutt* (Signature of Witness)

CERTIFICATE OF MAGISTRATE.

The Recruit above-named was cautioned by me that if he made any false answer to any of the above questions he would be liable to be punished as provided in the Army Act.
The above questions were then read to the Recruit in my presence.
I have taken care that he understands each question, and that his answer to each question has been duly entered as replied to, and the said Recruit has made and signed the declaration and taken the oath before me, at *Halifax* this *26* day of *November* 191 *7*

J W Logan Capt (Signature of Justice)

¶ I certify that the above is a true copy of the Attestation of the above-named Recruit.

A St Urbain Lt Col (Approving Officer)

M. F. W. 23.

After serving for two years, Private Elsworth Young was reported missing, arrested and returned to action. He fought for another two weeks, then was re-arrested, charged with desertion and executed by firing squad. This is his attestation paper, signed the day he enlisted at age nineteen.

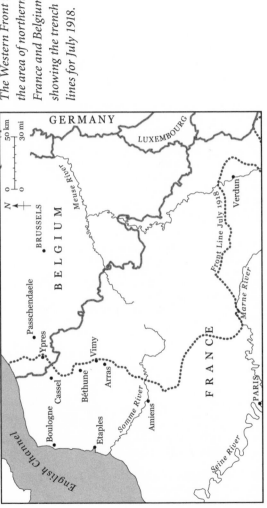

The Western Front in the area of northern France and Belgium, showing the trench lines for July 1918.

Acknowledgments

Grateful acknowledgment is made for permission to reprint the following:

Cover cameo: *George Herbert Casey of the 81st Infantry,* courtesy of Mary Frances Handley-Andrus.

Cover background: *29th Infantry Battalion advancing over "No man's land" through the German barbed wire and heavy fighting during the Battle of Vimy Ridge,* Capt. H.E. Knobel, Canada. Dept. of National Defence /Library and Archives Canada, PA-001020.

Cover details: Aged journal © sx70/istockphoto; aged paper © Shutterstock/Filipchuck Oleg Vasilovich; belly band © raplett/istockphoto; (back cover) label © Shutterstock/Thomas Bethge.

Page 187: *Piper James Cleland Richardson, V.C. (date of posthumous award 8 October 1916), 16th Battalion, C.E.F.,* Alexa Murray Collection/ Library and Archives Canada, C-033428.

Page 188: *Repairing trenches. 22nd Infantry battalion (French Canadian). July, 1916,* Library and Archives Canada, PA-000263.

Page 189: *Heavy howitzer in action,* W. I. Castle/Library and Archives Canada, PA-000743.

Page 190: *Personnel of the 16th Canadian Machine Gun Company holding the line in shell holes during the Battle of Passchendaele,* William Rider-Rider/Library and Archives Canada, PA-002162.

Page 191: *Canadian troops "going over the top" during training course at a trench-mortar school,* W.I. Castle/Canada. Dept. of National Defence/Library and Archives Canada, PA-000648.

Page 192: *Wounded Canadians on way to aid post. Battle of Passchendaele. November, 1917,* Canada. Dept. of National Defence/ Library and Archives Canada, PA-002107.

Page 193: *Wounded British Soldiers, taken in a churchyard which was used as a Dressing Station, July, 1916,* Library and Archives Canada, PA-000206.

Page 194: *Attestation paper of Private Elsworth Young,* Library and Archives Canada, RG 150, Accession 1992-93/166.

Page 195: Map by Paul Heersink/Paperglyphs.

The publisher wishes to thank Dr. Desmond Morton, author of *Marching to Armageddon, A Military History of Canada,* and *When Your Number's Up: The Canadian Soldier in the First World War,* for sharing his historical expertise, and Barbara Hehner for her careful checking of the factual details.

About the Author

John Wilson grew up surrounded by the evidence of war. He was born in 1951, a mere six years after the Second World War had ended. The stories he grew up with were of the fighter pilots in the Battle of Britain, prisoners of war escaping from Germany, and the men and women of the French Resistance blowing up railway lines and spying for the Allies. The stories were made more real when he discovered that he'd had an uncle who flew Spitfires and was shot down and lost over the English Channel in 1941. However, there was another war that gradually began to capture his interest.

On bicycle excursions around the Scottish countryside, John often found himself stopping for a cool drink beside a war memorial in some tiny village. The memorials sometimes showed a carved soldier, but more often than not were simple granite pillars upon which were carved the names of the soldiers from the area who had died. John soon noticed that, while there might be two or three names from the Second World War, there were usually ten times that number of names from an older war, often called The Great War or the War of 1914–1918.

This discovery, combined with the old, limping men who offered poppies on the street before Remembrance Day, triggered John's first foray into research. He read everything he could lay his hands on about this terrible event that had ended 33 years before he was born. A personal connection to the war was forged when he discovered that his wife's great-uncle, Richard Hay, had lied about his age in 1914 to join the army and been killed at the Battle of Loos in 1915. Richard's body was never found.

"Allan's experiences with Sommerfield's group of deserters is not based on an actual incident," John says, "but it is plausible. It is also an aspect of the war that deserves to be better known, if that is possible after all this time.

"Historical fiction takes what we know as historical truth, changes it as little as possible, and weaves a story through what we do not know. This is easy with, for example, an explorer who disappears mysteriously. In that case, the story needs to be true to what we know of the character and his or her time, but there is a large space in which a tale can be crafted. More often, the space is smaller and requires the weaving of a fictional story through the labyrinth of known historical events. Sometimes, as with *Shot at Dawn*, the space where some of the story occurs is a grey area where we do not know for sure what happened. In these cases, I was dealing with the possible and probable, but that is no reason not to undertake the endeavour. Not all historical truth — some would say very little — is accurately recorded in black and white."

John is the award-winning author of thirty books, both fiction and non-fiction and for various ages. All are about his primary interest, the past. The settings are the time of dinosaurs (the Weet Trilogy), Roman Legions (*Germania*), modern wars *(Four Steps to Death, Flames of the Tiger, Lost in Spain)* and coal mines on Vancouver Island *(Red Goodwin)*. He has revisited the First World War with both fiction — *And in the Morning* — and non-fiction — *Desperate Glory: The Story of WWI*. John's most recent novels are *Crusade: The Heretic's Secret, Book I*; *Death on the River*; *The Alchemist's Dream* and *Where Soldiers Lie*. In non-fiction, he has tackled the Second World War in *Bitter Ashes: The Story of WWII*. John's honours include a Governor General's Award nomination, four Geoffrey Bilson Award Honour Books, several Canadian Children's Book Centre Best Books for Teens, three Sheila Egoff Award Honour Books, three New York Public Library Best Books for Teens, and multiple shortlists for the White Pine, Red Maple, Snow Willow, Manitoba Readers' Choice, Chocolate Lily and Hackmatack Awards.

Other books in the
I AM CANADA Series

Prisoner of Dieppe
World War II
Hugh Brewster

Blood and Iron
Building the Railway
Paul Yee

For more information please see the I AM CANADA
website: www.scholastic.ca/iamcanada